"I look forward to [...] [...] maybe [...] for the holidays. I've never had a white Christmas."

"Really?" When she looked at him, her eyes sparkled with happiness. "I wasn't sure you would be staying that long."

"The truth is that I haven't figured out my future yet. I can't make you any promises."

"I never asked for one." Her eyes were flashing now but not with anything good. "What makes you think I want a commitment?"

"All I said was it would be nice to see snow. I honestly have no idea what I'm doing tomorrow so—"

"I'm not saying you have to decide. I made an innocent comment and you pushed back as if I suggested we elope next Sunday. I'm a big girl, Brendan—"

"Yeah. I noticed." Things would be less complicated if he hadn't.

She pushed away from the tree and faced him, standing just inches from him. This was not a good time to finally figure out what it meant that a woman was beautiful when she was angry. And Fiona was more beautiful than he'd ever seen her.

MONTANA MAVERICKS:
THE LONELYHEARTS RANCH:
You come there alone,
but you sure don't leave that way!

Dear Reader,

We've all heard the saying you can't go home again, but for some of us it's harder than others.

Growing up was rough for Brendan Tanner, but he finally found his niche in the Marine Corps. For the first time in his life he knew where he fit and his military family had his back. He loved his career... and then his father got sick. He resigned to take care of his dad only to lose the man who single-handedly raised him. Now he's more adrift than before. An invitation from an acquaintance to stay at Sunshine Farm in Rust Creek Falls offers him a place to stay while he gets back in shape—and considers reenlisting. But meeting beautiful Fiona O'Reilly may give him more than he bargained for!

Fiona has lived in Rust Creek Falls her whole life—which makes finding Mr. Right a challenge. Most of the guys in town feel like brothers. Taking a chance on a relationship with a stranger left her publicly humiliated, an experience not to be repeated. So now she's pushing thirty, feeling the pressure of being the oldest O'Reilly girl not yet married. One look at newcomer Brendan Tanner convinces her things might be looking up! If she can convince him that he belongs right where he is...

I hope you enjoy reading about how Fiona brings Brendan into the fold as much as I enjoyed writing their Montana Mavericks story.

Happy reading!

Teresa Southwick

Unmasking the Maverick

Teresa Southwick

Special thanks and acknowledgment to Teresa Southwick
for her contribution to the Montana Mavericks:
The Lonelyhearts Ranch continuity.

Recycling programs
for this product may
not exist in your area.

ISBN-13: 978-1-335-46602-0

Unmasking the Maverick

Copyright © 2018 by Harlequin Books S.A.

Printed in U.S.A.

Teresa Southwick lives with her husband in Las Vegas, the city that reinvents itself every day. An avid fan of romance novels, she is delighted to be living out her dream of writing for Harlequin.

Books by Teresa Southwick

Harlequin Special Edition

The Bachelors of Blackwater Lake

Just What the Cowboy Needed
His By Christmas
The New Guy in Town
Just a Little Bit Married
A Word with the Bachelor
How to Land Her Lawman
The Widow's Bachelor Bargain
A Decent Proposal
The Rancher Who Took Her In
One Night with the Boss
Finding Family...and Forever?

Montana Mavericks: The Baby Bonanza

Her Maverick M.D.

Montana Mavericks: What Happened at the Wedding?

An Officer and a Maverick

Montana Mavericks: 20 Years in the Saddle!

From Maverick to Daddy

Montana Mavericks: Back in the Saddle

The Maverick's Christmas Homecoming

Visit the Author Profile page
at Harlequin.com for more titles.

To the brave men and women of the United States military. Thank you for your service and sacrifice.

Chapter One

The poor kid from Prosperity, Texas, who hated fixing other people's trash for a living had come full circle.

On the upside, his father would be proud. But Brendan Tanner had a lot of mileage on him since those resentful teenage days. The Corps had a way of turning an ungrateful kid into a buttoned-up, battle-hardened marine. And it was the best thing that ever happened to him.

Now he was in Rust Creek Falls, Montana, fixing a broken toaster. He was living at a place called Sunshine Farm. After seeing something online about it being a welcome place to get a fresh start, he'd reached out to Luke Stockton, one of the owners, and the cowboy had invited him to stay as long as he wanted. The name made him smile, although the upward curving of his mouth felt a little rusty. In the last eighteen months there hadn't been much to smile about.

It disappeared when he heard a sudden high-pitched squeal. Those battle-hardened marine instincts kicked in and he automatically took a defensive stance, then realized the sound was a child's laughter. Slowly he released his breath. The reflexes were still sharp, but apparently so were the bad memories.

The kid in question burst through the open door of his temporary barn workshop and came to a stop in front of Brendan. The blond, blue-eyed little guy stared up at him and chewed on his index finger.

"Hey, buddy. Where's your mama? Did you go rogue?"

The kid babbled something that could have been a foreign language for all Brendan knew, then pointed to his tall rolling toolbox. It had belonged to his father, one of the few things he'd brought with him from Texas. When word got out that he was handy, he'd found a use for the tools. Something told him this kid could put them to use, too, but there would be hell to pay.

His next thought was all about heaven when the prettiest redhead he'd ever seen appeared in the workshop doorway.

"Jared! There you are, you little stinker." The reprimand was spoken with such affection that it wasn't a scolding at all. Then she smiled at Brendan. "Hi."

"Ma'am." He nodded and touched the brim of his Stetson. She was a little breathless, probably from running, but it was just about the sexiest thing he'd ever seen. "I wondered where his mom was."

"Oh, I'm not his mother. Aunt by marriage. My sister Fallon married Jamie Stockton, who was a widower, and she became a mom to his triplets—Jared, Henry and Kate."

Brendan watched her grab the kid when he made a move toward the toolbox. Instantly the boy started squirming to escape. If Brendan was in her arms, escape would be the last thing on his mind.

Then it sank in. Triplets. "There are two more like him?" he asked.

"Triple joy." She laughed and held on to the little wiggle worm. "Or triple trouble. It changes from moment to moment."

"Dat." Jared pointed a stubby little finger at a screwdriver sitting on the workbench. "Want dat."

The kid's determination increased his twisting to get free, but to her credit the redhead hung on. Brendan had trained in hand-to-hand combat in the Marines and wasn't sure he could have managed to wrangle the boy. He'd never been around kids, but even he knew giving this small human a sharp tool was a bad idea—no matter how determined he was to have it. He could offer to supervise, but there were too many ways for the situation to go sideways. Then he had an idea.

Underneath the workbench was a basket of broken toys. Eva Stockton, the wife of Luke, who owned Sunshine Farm, had given it to him. She'd said she kept them around for her niece and nephews and asked him to repair any he could. The kids were hard on them, she'd said, and after meeting Jared he understood what she meant.

He pulled the stash out into the open. "Maybe he'd like to look through these?"

"You're a lifesaver." The woman looked at him as if he'd hung the moon.

The lifesaver part was truer than she knew, Brendan thought. He'd saved lives, and buddies had saved his, too. They shared a bond unlike anything he'd ever known, the tight-knit family he'd never had. A brotherhood forged in battle. But a different sort of skirmish ensued when the redhead set little Jared on his feet. The toolbox was forgotten as he started in on the toys.

"Car!" Jared held one up that was missing a wheel. He squatted down and set it on the hard-packed clay floor and made the universal sound effect used by boys to simulate an engine revving.

"Here's to the short attention span of a two-and-a-half-year-old." The woman's eyes were big and blue and beautiful. The laughter shining there was really something special. "He hasn't seen those broken toys for so long they're like brand-new to him."

"I haven't had a chance to check them out and see if they're salvageable."

"Eva and Luke are keeping you busy?"

"Understatement. Fix a broken clothes dryer and suddenly you're a Jedi knight who can use the force to put Humpty Dumpty back together." He shrugged. "And they tell all their friends."

"So, do I call you Sir Jedi? Or do you have a name?"

He nearly winced. Obviously his social skills were as rusty as his smile. "Brendan Tanner."

She held out her hand. "Fiona O'Reilly."

He took her hand and something crackled up his arm, shocking the words right out of his head. He barely managed to mumble, "Nice to meet you."

While his brain was frozen, the rest of him was hot as a Texas sun on the hard-packed plains.

Before it turned awkward, Jared struck again. He'd emptied every last toy from the basket. Apparently the process of taking them out *was* playing with them and he was on to bigger and better things. Like the toolbox he'd temporarily forgotten. He opened a metal drawer, the one with various saw blades.

Without thinking it through, Brendan grabbed him up before he could touch anything and hurt himself. There was an instant screech of protest.

"I think they heard that in the next county." He looked at Fiona. "Sorry. Didn't mean to startle him, but those things are sharp."

"You have pretty good reflexes." Instead of being

upset, she looked impressed. The kid, however, was ticked off and held his arms out to her. She took him and ignored the loud grunts and the struggle to get back down. "No way, Jared. How come you don't know by now that I'm not a soft touch?"

Brendan begged to differ with her on that. She looked plenty soft to him, in all the right places. But he knew that was not what she meant. "I can't imagine herding two more like this one."

"That's why I'm here. Luke and Eva invited the family to dinner and I'm part of the reinforcements. Fallon has Henry. The last time I saw them he was chasing a chicken and she was hot on his heels. Jamie was keeping Kate from going headfirst into the horse's water trough. And I drew the short straw. We call him jackrabbit because he's so fast." She kissed his cheek and made smacking noises, getting a giggle out of the squirmy boy.

The sight of this woman with a child in her arms struck a chord deep inside Brendan. Her brightness flashed a light on the dark emptiness he carried around, the dusty place where he stored any hope of having a family.

"There you are." Luke Stockton walked into the workshop.

It was getting like Grand Central Station in here, Brendan thought. For some reason he didn't completely mind the invasion. He had liked Luke Stockton the first time they met and hadn't changed his mind since he'd been here at Sunshine Farm. His blue eyes projected honesty, integrity, and the deep tan was a result of hard outdoor work.

He shook hands with Brendan, then looked at Fiona and his nephew. "Your sister was getting worried. About you. And keeping up with Jared."

"Oh, please." Fiona rolled her eyes. "I'm onto this little man."

"I see you two have met," Luke said, glancing between her and Brendan.

"We introduced ourselves," she confirmed.

Luke took the squirming little boy, who was holding out his arms. Probably hoping this time he'd get put down. But Luke held him tight. "What are you up to, jackrabbit?"

"He's not happy," Fiona said. "Brendan wouldn't let him juggle the saw blades in his toolbox."

"You've got a mean streak," Luke teased.

"That's me. Making kids cry. It's a gift," Brendan said.

"Yeah. Speaking of gifts…" Luke looked at Fiona. "This guy can fix anything from a can opener to a car engine."

"So I heard." Fiona's eyes sparkled with amusement. "You're working him so hard the poor man hardly has time for anything else."

"Me?" Luke shook his head. "I just mentioned to a couple of people that he's got some skills repairing broken things. It's not my fault folks in Rust Creek Falls ran with it."

"So he should be flattered while working his fingers to the bone?" She folded her arms over her chest.

Luke lifted the wriggling kid above his head and got a snort of laughter out of him. "It's clear to any enterprising person that there's a need around here for this kind of service. I'm trying to talk him into opening a repair shop."

"And?"

Brendan noticed a questioning look in her eyes, along with something that might have been female interest. If he was right about that, the attraction was mutual. "And

I keep telling Luke that I will likely be gone in a few months."

"That's not a definite," the other man said. "I'm telling you there's money to be made and we need to spread the word."

"If there's one thing folks in Rust Creek Falls are good at, it's talking. It's almost a competitive sport around here," she joked.

"A business venture isn't the *only* reason to stick around." Luke glanced at Fiona, then back. "This is a close community with good people."

Brendan couldn't swear to it but he'd bet money that Fiona blushed.

All she said was, "This town has a charm, for sure."

And then another redhead appeared in the workshop doorway, holding an identical version of Jared. That must be Henry. And if the feather he was tightly clutching in his little fist was any indication, he'd caught up with that unfortunate chicken.

"See?" He held it up proudly.

"So the party is in here." This was Fallon Stockton.

Even if Brendan hadn't already met her, he would have guessed a sibling connection to Fiona just because of the coloring. She was pretty enough, but...she wasn't Fiona. And he was going to forget that thought had ever entered his mind.

"It is getting crowded in here," Luke agreed. "Also it's not a safe place to turn these little guys loose." Again he held up Jared, who squealed with delight.

"Eva sent me to find everyone. Dinner will be ready soon. We have to get the kids washed up," Fallon said.

"On it." Fiona took Jared. "Nice to meet you, Brendan."

"Likewise." Politely he touched the brim of his Stetson.

"You should join us for dinner," Luke said to him.

That caught him off guard. "I don't know…"

"Eva cooks enough to feed half of Rust Creek Falls. On top of that, Fiona brought her famous four-cheese macaroni dish and it is not to be missed."

"It's kind of last minute," he hedged.

"There's plenty of food," Fallon confirmed.

"Tell him, Fiona," Luke urged. "He hasn't lived until he's tried your homemade mac and cheese."

"I don't like to toot my own horn."

No one could accuse Brendan of picking up on social cues, but even he didn't miss the obvious matchmaking. Apparently neither did Fiona. The look on her face said she could cheerfully strangle Luke Stockton.

"I appreciate the offer," he said, "but I'm pretty busy here. I promised to have these things back in working order by tomorrow."

"Okay." Luke nodded. "If you change your mind, there will be a place set at the table for you."

"Thanks anyway."

A place at the table, he thought, watching them all walk away. A family thing. He hadn't experienced much of that in his life and it was probably better for everyone if he stayed away. And by "everyone" he meant Fiona. He'd seen the wary look on her face when he'd been invited. It was so different from her smile when he'd used a basket of broken toys to fix a toddler's tantrum. Damn it. He wanted to hang the moon for her again.

In battle it was an unwritten rule that you never left a man behind. But watching her leave made him feel as if someone was and he had a bad feeling that man was him.

At the house, Fiona made a dash for the bathroom to see just how bad she had looked for her meet and greet with the hunky new guy. Her worst suspicions were con-

firmed. The overall effect was almost as bad as if she'd
been mud wrestling. Come to think of it, chasing after
little Jared Stockton wasn't much different, but still…

Red hair had escaped her ponytail and hung around
her face. The freckles on her nose, which she hated more
than anything except the five extra pounds on her hips,
were like dots begging to be connected. It's what happened when a girl didn't put on makeup because, hey, it
was just family.

If the universe had given her a clue that she would meet
the best-looking man in Montana, she would have made
more of an effort to minimize her flaws. No wonder he'd
turned down the dinner invitation. That and Luke throwing her at the poor man.

Now that she had a little distance from the power of his
sex appeal, she could finally think straight. It was probably for the best that he hadn't come to dinner. The last
time someone pushed her at a man, things ended badly.
And that time it was public.

Fiona opened the bathroom door and nearly tripped
over Jared, who was waiting for her. She picked him up.
"Hey, bud, at least you love me."

"Wuv you." He put his hands on her cheeks and kissed
her.

"You're a heartbreaker in training, that's what you are.
Let's go help Aunt Eva and Uncle Luke get dinner on
the table."

With the child in her arms, Fiona walked down the
hall and found her way to the dining room. It was crawl-
ing with Stocktons. Altogether there were seven Stockton
siblings, but only four were here. The oldest, Luke, sat
at the head of the table next to his new wife, Eva Arm-
strong. Bella was a Jones now, married to her husband,
Hudson. Daniel Stockton and his wife, Annie, had a pre-

teen daughter, Janie. Last was Jamie, who was married to Fiona's sister Fallon.

The family had been split up after their folks died. In recent years they'd been coming back together, and these Sunday night dinners were important to all of them.

The dining room table was set for what looked like an army. Eva was directing everyone like a general executing a battle plan. The triplets were settled into booster chairs with Jamie and Fallon in between to oversee them. The other couples took their places, and Fiona was directed to one of the two empty seats at the end of the table. The Stocktons had one single male brother left and she had a bad feeling.

She sat next to the empty chair. "Is Bailey coming?"

Luke laughed at her question. "He was invited, of course, but politely declined."

"Politely?" His wife, Eva, sat at a right angle to him in the place closest to the kitchen. "I think he said something about preferring horses to people."

Bella sighed. "That's just it. We're not people. We're family."

"He's got some issues to work through." Jamie spooned peas onto Jared's and Kate's little plastic plates and passed the bowl to Fallon to serve Henry. "Give him time. He'll come around. When he meets the right woman."

Here we go, Fiona thought. She was a woman. She was nice. She was single and getting very close to the ripe old age of thirty. They'd better not ask why she wasn't married unless they wanted to unleash a redhead's legendary temper.

"So, who is the extra plate for, then?" Fallon asked.

"We have a guest staying in one of the cabins. Brendan Tanner," Eva explained. "He fixed our dryer and some other things here at Sunshine Farm. Luke invited him to dinner."

Just hearing his name made Fiona's stomach feel funny. Nervous and excited. In a "crushing on him" kind of way. It was time to shut down this topic. "He said he couldn't make it."

"I'm hoping he'll change his mind," Luke said. "The man saved us the cost of a new clothes dryer. The least we can do is feed him dinner." As if on cue, a knock on the front door interrupted him. "Come in."

A moment later Brendan Tanner walked inside and stopped cold when he saw everyone looking at him. "You didn't say the fifth infantry, third battalion would be here."

Funny, Fiona thought. She'd been thinking an army was coming, too, when she'd seen how many places were set at the table.

"Always room for one more." Luke waved him closer. "Sit there next to Fiona. Glad you changed your mind. We're ready for you."

Good for them, Fiona thought. She wasn't ready for this at all. And if the look on Tanner's face was anything to go by, he wasn't, either. But there was something in his green eyes when he looked at her, an intensity that made them glow. Heat pooled low in her belly and her hands started to shake when he walked over and sat down. She'd give him this—the man had courage.

And he showered, she thought. His damp, freshly combed hair was a clue, as was the fresh scent of soap that clung to his skin. He'd changed his clothes, too. The plaid snap-front shirt tucked into jeans highlighted his narrow hips and broad shoulders. Eye candy for sure.

And she'd been staring. *Oh, boy, say something bril-*

liant. She cleared her throat. "So, Brendan, what made you change your mind?"

"Macaroni and cheese."

"The one I made?" She was feeling a little tingly and flattered.

"Is there another one?"

"I don't think so."

He shrugged one of those broad shoulders. "It's one of my favorites. Box or scratch, count me in."

"I see." Her tingly feeling went up in smoke. "So any bozo could throw ingredients together and you'd be first in line."

"I— That's not exactly what I meant—"

She grinned. "Just kidding. But seriously. If the dish I made for this dinner doesn't bring tears to your eyes then something is very wrong with your taste buds."

He smiled, and the power of the look enveloped her in a sort of golden haze. It was a little like floating close to the sun all by herself. Bright and quiet—

She suddenly realized how quiet this room was in spite of the large group around the table. They were all staring at her and Tanner. She'd once been the center of attention at a social gathering, and the horrible memory had humiliation pouring through her now as it had then. That time it was about a man, too.

She felt as if she was living out a comedy sketch. In a noisy room when you said something embarrassing at the same moment everyone went silent and heard you. This was like that. Even the triplets, who could usually be counted on for sounds in a pitch only dogs could hear, were mirroring the adults around them and staring.

You could cut the awkwardness with a butter knife. Poor Mr. Tanner looked as if he wanted the earth to swallow him whole. She had to do something.

"I'm starving. Let's get the food going." Fiona started to grab her macaroni casserole, but it was as big as the state of Rhode Island. Instantly Brendan reached out and lifted it for her. She put some on her plate and his. "Thanks."

"You're welcome."

As if a switch had been flipped, everyone was taking food and passing platters around. Attention had been successfully diverted away from them.

Her relief was a little premature because when everyone had filled their plates it got quiet again. She said the first thing that popped into her mind. "So, Brendan, where did you learn to fix things?"

He finished chewing and swallowed before answering. "My dad taught me."

"He must be very proud of you," Fiona said.

"He was. He passed away not too long ago."

"I'm sorry." The words were automatic and felt so inadequate when a sort of sad, haunted look slipped into his eyes.

"Thanks."

"I haven't seen anything that Brendan can't repair," Luke said. "Your dad must have been a good teacher, and the skill he gave you is invaluable."

Brendan looked thoughtful. "Funny you should say that. We didn't have much, but dad's knack for patching up what people threw out or paid him to fix put food on the table."

"An honest living," one of the men said.

"I suppose." He looked down at the full plate of food in front of him. "Necessity was the mother I didn't have."

It was like a curiosity bomb went off in Fiona's head. Follow-up questions exploded in her mind. But one of the triplets—Jared—made a bomb of his own and Fallon excused herself to change him.

The moment for interrogation passed when Hudson started talking to Brendan about horses. In Rust Creek Falls, that was like guys discussing cars anywhere else. It turned out that Brendan had worked on ranches in Texas for extra money. Was there anything he couldn't do?

That wasn't something she was going to ask. The less she knew about Brendan Tanner the better. She would bet he had a sad story, one that would engage her emotions. But he was a stranger and by his own admission was only in town temporarily. Matchmakers could throw them together until hell wouldn't have it but they couldn't make her play along.

Not again.

Chapter Two

Last night's dinner ranked up there as one of the best meals Brendan ever had. He'd eaten enough to feed a whole platoon. The Stocktons were friendly and caring folks who opened their farm to a stranger looking for a fresh start and they kept on giving. He was grateful for that. If not for Fiona O'Reilly, he could check off every box of a perfect evening.

It was bad enough that she made the best macaroni and cheese he'd ever tasted, but she was also the sexiest mac-and-cheese maker he'd ever met. Her eyes were beautiful. That curvy body had him itching to touch her. And her smile promised heaven at the same time it sent him to hell. All night.

When he hadn't tossed and turned from thinking about her, he'd been dreaming about having her in his bed. She was whip smart and wickedly funny, which was an irresistible combination. It meant danger up ahead, but only if he chose to go down that road. All he had to do was take a detour and avoid her.

That took care of his conscious mind. With luck the warning would filter down to his subconscious and keep her out of his dreams. He was a tumbleweed and she had deep roots here in Montana. Smart money was on sticking to his plan: get back in shape and reenlist in the Marine Corps where he belonged.

After an early morning run and workout, he went to the barn. Sunshine Farm made no demands on its guests but Brendan hated feeling useless and had gotten in the habit of helping feed the stock every morning. Today was no exception. He walked into the stable and grabbed a pitchfork to help spread hay for the horses.

Luke walked over and jammed his own long-handled tool into the bale. "Morning."

"Back at you."

"Glad you decided to join us for dinner last night. Any regrets?"

A few. None of which he'd talk about. "Best meal I've had in a long time."

"Did I lie about the macaroni and cheese?"

"No." Last night he'd been full and had still taken another helping. Eating for pleasure, which included the pleasure of rubbing elbows with the lady who'd made it.

"So, what do you think of Fiona?"

What did he think? Brendan was pretty sure that he was thinking about her more than he should be, and in ways that he didn't want to. "I think she makes a mean macaroni."

"Seriously? That's it?"

"What else?" He sighed. "She seems nice."

"I think she's interested in you," Luke commented. "Looked to me like there was a sparkle in her eyes when she stole glances at you."

She was stealing glances at him? That didn't suck. Then he shook his head. "You're imagining things."

"Nope. Eva saw it, too."

"You talked to your wife about this?"

"We talk about everything. She's my best friend, and then some," Luke said. "Besides, in Rust Creek Falls, talking and spreading news is how we roll."

He remembered Fiona saying something like that. "I think you're both imagining things."

"I disagree."

"For the sake of argument, let's say you're right. The question is, why me? I'm boring."

"You're new in town and single. And—don't take this the wrong way—but you're not a bad-looking guy."

"Stop. I'm blushing." The corners of his mouth curved up.

Luke laughed. "And Fiona is single, too."

"A woman who looks like her must have men lined up around the block."

"Not so much."

Brendan stuck his pitchfork in the bale of hay and leaned on it as he looked at the other man. "Why?"

"You'll have to ask her that."

No, he wouldn't be asking her anything, because it was unlikely there would be an opportunity to do that. "None of my business."

"That could change."

He grabbed the tool again, then forked up some hay and spread it in a nearby stall. "I don't think so."

"Time will tell."

After that the two of them worked in silence until all the horses were taken care of. Brendan knew from being on ranches in Texas that these animals had small stomachs relative to their size and needed to be fed two to three times a day to maintain their weight. He made it a point to be around when that happened.

"Any other chores I can help with?" he asked.

Luke didn't miss a beat before saying, "You can give

serious consideration to opening a repair business here at Sunshine Farm."

"You're persistent. I'll give you that."

His friend smiled. "There is something. In a couple of days my brother Jamie is rounding up cattle from their summer grazing spot in the hills and bringing them back for the winter. I'm giving him a hand but he could use another man. You game? He'd be appreciative."

"Glad to."

"Good. Thanks."

"Least I can do." Brendan sincerely meant that. He was grateful to be here and wanted to give back. There was something about this sunshine-yellow barn that brightened the dark places inside him.

Luke left shortly after that and Brendan went to his temporary shop in the barn. On the worktable was a food processor he'd started to take apart yesterday, before impulsively giving in to Luke's dinner invitation. The lady who dropped it off was annoyed that it crapped out right after the warranty was up. She didn't give the thing much of a chance at a second life and told him not to waste too much time trying. The thing was, after his morning workout he had nothing but time.

He removed a couple of small screws to separate the outer casing from the motor in order to assess the problem. Just as he was pulling it apart, his cell phone rang. He tapped the answer icon.

"Hello."

"Hey, it's Fiona O'Reilly."

"Oh. Hi." His voice sounded rusty but he resisted the urge to clear his throat.

"Hi." She hesitated a moment. "How are you?"

"Fine," he lied. Hearing her voice brought back visions

of her red hair and the teasing smile that had tension curling in his gut. "You?"

"Great." Her voice sounded rusty, too, but she cleared her throat. "So, dinner last night was good."

"Yeah. I'm not used to a spread like that."

"If you stick around long enough, the calories will catch up to you." She laughed ruefully. "I carry the proof of that on my hips."

In his opinion her hips were perfect, along with the rest of her. But saying so seemed out of line. "I added an extra couple of miles to my morning run."

"Speaking of running," she said, "last night you disappeared after clearing the table and just before dessert. A less secure woman might think you were trying to get away from her."

He had been, but not for the reason she probably thought. She was equal parts temptation and complication. Marines believed retreat wasn't an option but he'd made an exception for her. Because he'd also been trained in survival.

"If I'd stayed any longer, I'd have had another helping of everything and that would've just been embarrassing."

"Yeah. Eva outdid herself. She does the baking at Daisy's Donuts, but she's an all-around outstanding cook, too."

"I found that out." He waited for her to say something and when there was silence, he thought he'd lost her. "Fiona?"

"I'm here." She cleared her throat again. "I have something to ask you."

He frowned. Was it something he'd said at dinner? His remark about necessity being the mother he never had was one he wanted back in a big way. Bracing himself, he said, "Okay."

"I was wondering if you could bring your fix-anything

reputation out for a spin to my place and look at the tractor here on the ranch."

Part of him wanted to say "no way," but another part was ready to get there as fast as he could. Still, he was a civilian, a guest here, and that meant he needed to be especially polite to everyone because he owed the Stocktons.

"Look, Fiona, I don't know if I'm the right guy—"

"Just a quick look. My dad usually can repair the ranch machinery but he's stumped. I've called a repair shop in Kalispell but they can't send someone for close to a week. It's already October and winter is coming. There are time and weather-sensitive projects pending. You'd really be doing me a favor if you could swing by."

That is a really bad idea, he thought. "I don't know if that's possible…" He let the words hang there, hoping she'd bail him out.

After several moments, she sighed. "That's okay. It was just a thought. Apparently Luke mentioned to my father that you were handy with mechanical stuff and Dad asked me to call. But don't worry about it. We'll make do. Thanks anyway. I know you're really busy."

The disappointment in her voice grabbed him and wouldn't let go. It felt like he'd just turned his back on a helpless kitten. Damn, hell and crap. "I'm not that busy. I'll give it a look."

"Really? I appreciate it so much. Thanks."

He got directions, said he'd be right over, then disconnected the call and saved her number to his phone, shaking his head and muttering to himself. Suddenly Fiona O'Reilly had become his business and it ticked him off that Luke had been so right, so soon.

Fiona waited for Mr. Fix-it on the front porch. The interior of the O'Reilly family's rambling ranch house wasn't big enough for her and the nerves jumping around inside her. She hadn't expected to see him at all and definitely not this soon. It made her wonder if fate was taking a page from Luke Stockton's matchmaking book or just having a laugh at her expense.

She saw a black F-150 truck turn off the main road and head toward the house. That was a cue for the nerves to stop the jumping jacks, pull together and form a knot in her stomach. Why was she being such a twit? He was just another guy and didn't even want to be here. She'd practically twisted his arm and he was simply doing it as a favor because she'd played the "Dad asked me to call you" card. Paddy O'Reilly would survive if Brendan had said no. But Brendan didn't know that and now she had to see him.

The truck stopped in front of her and she noticed his Texas license plate in a United States Marine Corps frame. Pulling her denim jacket tighter against the chilly north wind, she left the porch to meet him as he exited the truck. Then he grabbed a red toolbox from the rear bed.

"Hey, thanks for coming."

"No problem." Politely he touched the brim of his Stetson. "If you'll point me in the right direction, I'll take a look at the tractor."

"Can I get you a cup of coffee or anything? I've got an extra to-go mug. My father and brothers, Ronan and Keegan, use them all the time." She was babbling and he was letting her. It wasn't easy but she stopped talking.

"No coffee. Thanks anyway."

"Okay. The tractor is parked in the shed down there next to the stable."

"This is a nice spread," he said as they walked. "I saw the sign as I drove in. Rusty Bucket Ranch. Interesting name."

"Kind of whimsical but down to earth." She smiled up at him. "My ancestors emigrated from Ireland. They made their living from the land and wanted to do that in America. So they came West and found this property. After buying it, as the tale goes, they had nothing left but a rusty bucket. The name stuck."

"And they prospered."

"Yeah. We have all this." She gazed from the white, split rail corral fence and stable to the other ranch buildings and the barn her brothers had converted into their living space. "And a tractor that won't start."

"Let's see what we can do to change that." He followed her into the shed.

"You can set your toolbox on the worktable there." She went to the other end and opened the doors to give him more light, then came back. Her breath caught when she saw that he'd removed his long-sleeved flannel shirt. The olive green T-shirt he wore under it was snug and fit him like a second skin that highlighted every luscious muscle.

She swallowed, then said, "So, here she is. Sorry about the tool explosion there. My dad left all his stuff out. He was going to take another look at it. Just between you, me and the goats, that would involve less looking and a lot more colorful language. When he's working on this tractor, the words run more to the four-letter variety."

While she nattered on, he'd opened the side panel to inspect the inside. Without looking up, he said, "What about you?"

"Oh, I've been known to swear, but only when necessary. And always in a ladylike way." She heard him chuckle and that brought a smile to her face. Resting her back against the workbench, she settled in to keep him company. Hand him tools. Admire the way his back muscles moved and bunched under that snug shirt. Check out his world-class butt in the worn jeans. "And I guess I also have a way with words that are more than four letters."

"How's that?" He didn't look up but kept poking around in the tractor engine.

"I write freelance articles about ranch life for farm and outdoor magazines."

"What kind of articles?"

"A recent one was about recycling bent nails, rusty hinges and old bottles. A rancher's motto is 'Use it up, wear it out, make it do or do without.'"

"I know all about that," he said wryly.

She remembered him saying he'd grown up making do. "I'm working on an article now about preparing for the winter. Cold weather in Montana isn't for sissies."

"I bet."

"So, between my writing job and chores on the ranch, I keep pretty busy."

"Sounds like it. A good life."

"It is. I love what I do."

"You're lucky."

She couldn't see his expression but there was a wistful tone in his voice. Since he had his head buried in the engine, this might be a good time to ask some of the questions that had been rolling around in her mind when she couldn't sleep last night.

She'd hoped he would open up a little while ago when she called, but he didn't. Maybe he would now. What was the worst that could happen? He'd take his tools and go home? She was willing to risk it.

"So, dinner last night was awkward. Did you notice how we got paired off?"

"Yup." He still didn't look at her. "This morning when I was helping with chores, Luke asked what I thought about you."

"No. Really? What did you say?" That was unexpected.

"I told him you make a mean macaroni."

And? Her heart skipped a beat waiting for...what? Didn't matter because he didn't come through with more. "At least you didn't say *I* was mean."

"Actually, I said you seem nice."

"I think I am. But Luke was probably just making polite conversation. Not necessarily matchmaking."

"There's more. He underlined the fact that you're single and I'm single."

"And?" she prompted.

"And I asked him why you're still single."

"What did he say?"

"That I should ask you. So, why are you still single?"

"Because I'm not married," she said.

"Smart-ass. So why aren't you married?"

If that question had come up at dinner last night she would have been angry and defensive. With so many people watching her reaction, it would have felt too much like the public way she'd found out the man she'd expected a proposal from had cheated on her and gotten a girl pregnant. But now they were alone, and Brendan wasn't even looking at her, so it felt like the solitude of the confessional.

"So many reasons for being single," she started. "I'm too old—pushing thirty, a spinster by Old West standards. Not thin enough. Men seem to like stick women who have to run around in the shower to get wet. On top of that there are no men here in Rust Creek Falls—"

"Don't look now but—" Without turning he lifted a greasy hand. "Man. Says so right on my driver's license."

"Okay. That last one deserves some context. I grew up in Rust Creek Falls. Spent my whole life here and most of the guys have, too. They're friends of Ronan and

Keegan and, by extension, like my brothers. So…ew. It's too weird. That makes meeting men a challenge."

"Okay. I respect your honesty." He glanced over his shoulder. "Luke was just doing his part, then."

"Exactly." She beamed at him. "Look at you paying attention and participating in the conversation."

"I've been told I'm too quiet. So I've been making an effort since I got out."

By "out" she assumed he meant leaving the military. Since he was doing his best to take part, she'd give him an opportunity to share. Maybe the fact that he was elbow-deep in a tractor engine would help.

"I noticed your license plate holder. So you were a marine?"

"Yup. From Prosperity, Texas." He picked up a tool from the workbench beside him. "I loved the Corps. It was a good career."

She could hear respect, reverence and regret in his tone. And, frankly, he sounded a little lost. "Why did you leave, then?"

"My dad got sick. Cancer. I came home to be with him."

"That must have been a difficult time. I bet you miss him."

His movements stilled for a moment. "Yeah."

Fiona knew about Luke and Eva's plan to offer a stay at Sunshine Farm to someone going through a hard time in order to pay their happiness and good luck forward. They were always looking for someone in need of a fresh start. With these bits of information Brendan had revealed, she could see why they'd opened their arms to him. "So you're trying to figure out what to be when you grow up?"

He didn't answer but straightened from his trouble-shooting position over the engine and climbed up on the

tractor. The key was in the ignition and he turned it. Instantly the engine rumbled to life. He nodded. Anyone
else would have pumped their arm or woo-hooed in tri-
umph. A victory boot scoot wouldn't be out of the question, either. But not this man. His reaction was quiet
satisfaction.

He turned off the machine and climbed down. "Mission accomplished."

"What did you do?"

"There were some wires way down in the belly, hard
to see, right next to the housing for—"

She held up a hand to stop him. "My head will explode
if you say one more word."

"Okay." He grinned as he grabbed a rag and wiped the
worst of the grease off his hands.

The look was so darn cute it liquefied her brain cells.
That's when she realized talking to him without eye contact was much easier. *Pull it together, Fiona*, she told
herself. "If my dad wants to know what you did I'll just
have him call you."

"Okay."

"Seriously, though, thank you so much. Come on up to
the house and I'll give you a check for your work. What
do I owe you?"

Without missing a beat he said, "Dinner."

That surprised her. This was business and usually that
involved taking payment for one's work. So maybe she'd
misunderstood. "I'd be happy to buy you dinner, but—"

He shook his head. "A gentleman would never let a
lady pay. I want to buy you dinner."

She almost blurted out, "Shut the front door," but managed to hold back. "Let me get this straight. You fixed my
dad's tractor and want to take me to dinner as payment?"

"Yes. Tomorrow night. On one condition."

"What?" she asked, a little suspicious now.

He grabbed his flannel shirt, slung it over his broad shoulder by one finger and met her gaze. "Just you and me. No family."

He wanted to be alone with her? *Pinch me*, she thought. This had to be a dream. A handsome man, single and sexy, was asking her out to dinner? This was shocking. She'd been so sure he was running away from her last night.

"Fiona?"

"Oh. Right." She smiled. "I'd like that very much."

"Then I'll pick you up at six thirty. Is that okay?"

Heck, yes. But all she said was, "That would be fine."

What in the world was she going to wear?

Chapter Three

What had he been thinking?

"Tanner, you're an idiot. Asking the woman to dinner. In payment for services rendered, no less." And now he was talking to himself. The downward spiral into hell was picking up speed and momentum.

His father must be turning over in his grave about this. He could just hear it. *That's no way to make a living. Since when do we not take money for our work?*

Since the woman he did the work for looked like Fiona. That smile… When the tractor engine sputtered to life, she'd looked at him again as if he'd hung the moon. A man could get used to that.

"Knock, knock."

Brendan turned away from his workbench and saw an older woman standing in the doorway. She was probably in her sixties, not very tall and had shoulder-length silver hair. There was spitfire in her eyes and a blender in her arms.

She moved closer and looked up at him. "Are you Brendan Tanner?"

"Yes, ma'am."

She held out her hand. "Edna Halstead."

"Nice to meet you."

"Same here. Luke Stockton says you can fix anything."

"I wouldn't say that, but I'm pretty good at repairs." He nodded at the small appliance she was holding. "Having trouble with that?"

"Blasted thing just quit. They don't make things like they used to. It's practically new."

"That's always the way. I'll see what I can do."

She handed it over. "Just when I got my husband to drink protein shakes, too."

"I'm guessing he'd be just as happy if I couldn't fix this." He put the base and pitcher on the workbench then looked back at her still staring at him. "Was there something else?"

"Mind looking at it now? I'd rather not make another trip out here. Unless you're too busy…"

"No, ma'am."

"Good. I wouldn't expect it would take long. It isn't the space station. If it's a goner, I expect you'll know that right away."

"Yeah." He picked up a small screwdriver to take apart the base.

"I don't expect a lifetime warranty," she said. "Still, you should get a little more time out of something."

"Yes, ma'am."

"It's not expensive to get another one, but just on general principle I don't want to do that."

"No, ma'am." He checked out all the connections and the cord, then cleaned and tightened anything that looked to be loose while the woman chattered away.

"The thing is, my husband, J.T., and I are retired and on a fixed income, so we have a budget."

"Understood."

"Are you military, Mr. Tanner?"

"Was." And he missed it, even more after losing his dad. He missed his brothers. Missed doing work that was important. Now he had no mission, no focus except to be in the best possible physical shape for reenlisting.

"What branch of the service?" Her eyes glittered with interest.

"Marine Corps."

"*Semper fi.* Your service is much appreciated and welcome home."

"Thank you." He stopped working and met her gaze. "Were you in the military?"

She shook her head. "Only by marriage. J.T. was a marine."

"Vietnam?"

"Did my age give it away?" she teased.

"No, ma'am. What is it they say? Fifty is the new forty?"

She laughed. "I'm a little north of that. Almost seventy. And you know it."

"Doesn't show. And what I know is a lot of service members who served their country during that conflict were never properly welcomed home. That wasn't right."

"No." Her mouth pulled tight for a moment. "Since then folks have learned to separate service to country from politics. Hopefully that will never happen again. Some make the ultimate sacrifice. Others live with physical disabilities."

Something in her expression said she knew about that. "Your husband?"

"He lost a leg—above the knee."

"Sorry to hear that, ma'am."

"Stop calling me that. 'Ma'am' makes me feel like I lived through the Revolutionary War. Edna, Ed or Eddie will do."

"Yes, ma—" He saw her glare and stopped. "Eddie."

"Good choice." She grinned. "And don't be feeling sorry for J.T. He's taken it in stride, if you'll pardon the pun. He's one tough marine. The few—"

"The proud. The Marines," he finished.

"Oorah."

He closed up the blender base. "There's no real obvious sign of trouble. I tightened a few loose wires and made sure the rest was shipshape. Let's plug it in and see."

"Sure do hope you're as good as Luke claims."

"Here goes." He saw her cross her fingers.

He plugged in the blender and with one last look at her he pushed a button. The thing came to life and the woman smiled her appreciation.

"Looks like you're back in the protein shake business," he told her. "Hope your husband is happy, too."

"He'd rather have his bacon, eggs and fried potatoes. But we have a deal. A healthy breakfast earns a scoop of ice cream after dinner."

"Seems fair."

"He doesn't think so but we both know who the commanding officer is."

"Skipper." Brendan saluted. "Only an idiot would mix it up in a skirmish like that."

"Speaking of idiots…" There was a gleam in her eyes. "What woman did you ask to dinner?"

He froze. "What?"

"You were mumbling to yourself about it when I came in."

"You heard that?" he asked.

"It's a popular misconception that all old people are hard of hearing. For the record, there's nothing wrong with my ears. You apparently are having second thoughts about asking a woman to dinner. So I'd like to know what woman we're talking about and I can tell you whether or not you're right about being an idiot."

He already knew he was. He momentarily toyed with the idea of saying *we* weren't talking about anything, but something told him Eddie Halstead would have a big problem with that response.

"I fixed a tractor at the Rusty Bucket Ranch earlier today and—"

"Fiona O'Reilly." It took her all of a second and a half to put it together.

"How did you know?"

"You don't seem the type to hit on a married woman. Her sisters, Fallon and Brenna, are. To Jamie Stockton and Travis Dalton respectively." She nodded firmly. "Since Fiona is the last single O'Reilly daughter and lives on the Rusty Bucket Ranch, she must be the woman in question."

"You're not wrong."

"And you're not an idiot," she said. "Why would you think so? She's beautiful, smart and dependable."

"It's complicated."

"Bravo Sierra," she snapped, using marine slang for BS. "That just means you don't want to talk about it."

She was dead-on about that. "Look, if it's all the same to you—"

"Eddie Halstead." Luke walked in and gave the older woman a big hug. "I saw your car outside and had to come and say hello."

"Good to see you, Luke." She glanced at Brendan. "You were right about him. He fixed my blender."

"So, J.T. will be back in the business of drinking his breakfast," the rancher guessed.

"A shake is healthier than bacon and eggs," she said stubbornly. "Especially if he's going to keep up with his chores."

"Eva would agree with that."

"And my stubborn man isn't getting any younger. He's got arthritis in his hands and one good leg. These days, climbing on a ladder is like a combat mission." She looked from Brendan to Luke. "He's pretty handy but I don't like him on a ladder. Ladder fall figures increase with age and physical condition. The man is sixty-eight years old, although you wouldn't know it to look at him. Don't tell him I said that. The point is, he's too old to be on a ladder even if he had two good legs. Gonna make putting up Halloween decorations a challenge this year."

"I'd be happy to help out." Brendan looked at her. "Say the word and I'll swing by."

"Come to think of it," she said as she tapped her lip. "The refrigerator is making a funny noise."

"Make a list," he said.

"I would sure appreciate it. The thing is, J.T.'s proud, if you get my drift."

"Sure do," Brendan said. "But if he gives you any trouble, just tell him it's one marine helping out a brother."

"I don't want to take up your time," she said.

"He's got plenty to spare," Luke interjected.

"Seems so," Eddie said. "He just fixed the O'Reilly's tractor and instead of taking money he's taking Fiona out to dinner."

"Well, well." Luke grinned. "All because of a house call."

"Marines work fast," the older woman said.

Luke snapped his fingers. "I just had an idea. You could expand the repair shop and go mobile with it. For the things people can't drop off."

"Now why would I want to do that?" Brendan asked.

"Because making money is a good thing," Eddie said.

"Unless you ask all of your customers to dinner. Then you're flirting with a negative cash flow."

"Understood," Brendan told her. "But that's not what I meant. I don't want to make long-term plans."

"How's that?" she asked.

"Because I'm only here temporarily."

"Why?" she asked. "You have somewhere better to be?"

That's what he was here to figure out.

No matter how many times she reminded herself that Brendan wasn't staying permanently, Fiona couldn't tamp down her excitement to see him. Telling herself this wasn't a date didn't help, either. For some reason it was how he was taking payment for fixing the tractor.

And that was where her thought process went off the rails. He wouldn't accept money but wanted to take her to dinner. Maybe he wanted more than that, but she didn't think so. If that didn't go to a girl's head, she was the Queen of England. The logical conclusion was that he wanted to see her. Alone. Without family.

And she was stoked.

She'd even bought a new dress—a hunter green, long-sleeved knit that minimized her curves even as it hugged them. A contradiction that paralleled the coming social occasion she refused to call a date. The dress's hem teased the top of her new low-heeled, knee-high black leather boots. They were a splurge, but when she got paid for her latest article, her budget would be just fine. Tonight it was important to look like a woman, not a ranch hand.

She checked out her appearance in the full-length, free-standing mirror in her bedroom, the one she used to share with Fallon and Brenna. There were times, like now, when she missed her sisters being around to tell her whether or not the neckline of this dress was too plain and begged for jewelry. If her hair was too curly, too straight or just right. Did her newly perfected smoky eye make her look like a hooker?

Brenna would always flop on the bed and give her two cents. *You look too prudish. Lower the neckline, shorten the skirt. Show more skin. A little cleavage couldn't hurt.*

Fiona turned from side to side, studying the way the soft material clung to her breasts. "Make him wonder about what he can't see," she told her reflection.

The first time they met she'd looked like a pig wrestler. Yesterday she'd had time to brush her hair and put on some tinted sunscreen along with sheer lip gloss. Tonight she was going for something between demure and dynamite. Just to show him she could. If only her sisters were here to confirm that she'd pulled it off.

Fiona glanced at the clock beside her bed and her heart skipped a beat. He would be here soon. There was still time to tone it down if her mother thought she'd gone too far.

Grabbing her heavy wool shawl and black clutch purse, she headed downstairs, where Maureen O'Reilly was fixing dinner. The kitchen was a big, open room with lots of counter space, a farm sink and a big round oak table with eight chairs. Years ago, when all of them had been under one roof, they'd totaled seven.

Now, Fallon and Brenna were happily married and sharing living space with their respective husbands. Her older brothers, Ronan and Keegan, had bachelor quarters here on the ranch where they worked. The two showed no sign of settling down and it worked for them. Her mother was thrilled to have them close by.

Maureen was checking something in the oven, then straightened and turned when she heard Fiona's footsteps on the wood floor. "Hey, sweetie. You look beautiful. That emergency shopping trip yesterday afternoon really paid off."

Fiona looked down at the slightly flared skirt and smoothed her palms over her hips. Unlike Fallon and Brenna, their mother might sugarcoat her opinion.

"You don't think it's too—"

"It's not *too* anything." She set pot holders on the counter beside the pot simmering on the stove. "Not too dressy, just casual enough."

That had been the challenge since Fiona didn't know where they were going to dinner. "Really?"

"Yes."

The back door opened and in walked her tall, handsome, brown-haired, blue-eyed brothers. Women were drawn to them like dieters to donuts. And both stopped dead in their tracks when they saw her.

Ronan, the oldest, whistled. "Look at you. Got a hot date?"

Brendan was hot, but this wasn't technically a date. "I'm going out."

"With who?" Keegan asked.

"No one you know," she hedged.

"How do you know who we know?" her oldest brother challenged her.

Instead of answering, Fiona blew out a breath and met her mother's gaze. "Why are they here?"

"It's pot roast night," Keegan said, as if that explained why these two, who often fended for themselves, had shown up for dinner.

"So what?" She knew she sounded like a ten-year-old, but it couldn't be helped. The knuckleheads would not help get her to a Zen place before Brendan showed up. In fact, they'd do just the opposite. "Mom could fix pheasant under glass and the two of you couldn't be counted on to put in an appearance."

"Are we unreliable?" Ronan asked his mother.

"Yes."

He walked over and affectionately slid his arm across her shoulders. "Am I still your favorite?"

"I do not have favorites where my children are concerned. I can, however, confirm that you are still the oldest of five."

"And Fiona is the oldest girl." There was a teasing gleam in Keegan's eyes that women seemed to find adorable, if Rust Creek Falls gossip was anything to go by. "She's the only one of my sisters still here for dinner. Oh, wait, she's wearing a dress. The world has gone crazy."

"I've changed my mind—" she started to say before Keegan interrupted her.

"Along with your tomboy look."

"It's official," she said. "Brenna isn't the dramatic one. You are."

"I'm Irish." Keegan grinned. He was awfully cute when he did that. "Drama is a badge of honor."

"And so is being good with words," Ronan pointed out. "Which you are, sis. You've verbally danced around the question of who you are going out with. Now, fess up. Who did you put on a pretty new dress for tonight?"

"What are you? The fashion police? You don't know that it's new." Since when did he get hit with the observant stick?

"You're deflecting again," he countered. "This could be serious."

"Or, to say it a different way," Keegan chimed in, "what poor, unsuspecting guy are you trying to snag?"

"That's ridiculous," she countered.

"Is it?" He arched an eyebrow and held up three fingers while he ticked off his reasons. "Oldest girl. Still not married. Pushing the big three-oh."

"I'd like to push you off a cliff," she mumbled. "And for your information, not that you deserve any consideration, but I am not looking for a husband. I don't need one to enjoy a full and happy life."

"That's very enlightened of you." Keegan nodded approvingly. "I could have told you that. All you had to do was ask."

"Can we talk about the fact that you're alone?" Fiona made a scoffing sound. "Because, judging by your track record, you are the very last person I would take advice from."

"Why me?" There was mock innocence on her brother's face. "Ronan is the one who set you up with Tate Gibbs."

A new guy in town that he'd met at Ace in the Hole, the local cowboy bar. The jerk had turned out to be a liar and cheat.

She noticed a guilty expression on her oldest brother's face. In spite of her annoyance with these two, she didn't want him to feel bad about what happened. Ultimately she'd made the choice to fall for her ex. It was her own bad judgment that got her heart broken. Lesson learned.

"I'm not looking to get married," she said firmly. "I've stopped looking for a man. Period."

"Keep an open mind, honey." Up until now their mother had stayed out of the verbal volley and simply listened. Now, though, she stepped in. "When you least expect it, that's when love will happen. When you've stopped looking, it will find you."

Another tired saying that should be stitched on a sampler and hung on the wall. Fiona envied her parents' thirty-plus years of marriage. They were still happy and deeply in love, stealing kisses like teenagers when they thought no one was watching. More than once someone would teasingly tell them to get a room. But that kind of love was exactly what she wanted. It just didn't seem as if it was in the cards for her. And there was no way she'd settle for less.

Brendan Tanner was intriguing, she would give him that. And there was something inherently heroic about him. The way he'd handled little Jared with patience and kindness spoke to how he would be with kids of his own. And the fact that he was taking her to dinner instead of letting her pay him to fix the tractor made him seem like a really good man. But she'd been wrong before.

He was basically another stranger in town and she was definitely against getting burned again. He was certainly a pretty package and she was curious about him. But her only goal was one nice evening out.

Before she could tell the boys to go jump in the lake, the back door opened again and her father walked in, followed by his dog, Duchess. Paddy O'Reilly was a big, handsome man and his sons took after him. That was even more painfully clear when he stopped and stared at her the way they had.

"No one told me we were dressing up for dinner tonight," he said, absently rubbing the dog's golden head.

"Fiona's not eating here," Maureen told him.

"She has a date but won't tell us who she's going out with," Keegan informed his father.

"Whoever he is, he's a very lucky man." Paddy's eyes were filled with paternal pride. "You're the image of your mother and she had the men falling all over themselves for a chance with her."

"Thanks, Dad." Fiona felt a lump in her throat.

"So who is this fortunate fella?" His eyes twinkled, proof he knew he wasn't fooling her. Information was what he wanted. "Are we going to have an opportunity to meet him?"

"Not if I can help it."

Oh, dear God. He would be here any minute and she wanted to spare him the awkward family once-over. Now the guardians of the Galaxy were standing shoulder to shoulder, ready to grill the guy. The poor man had done them a favor and this was how they repaid him!

With her shawl and purse in hand, she turned on her heel and hurried to the living room, planning to slip out the door. But the plan was doomed to failure and if she wasn't so darn nervous that would have been clear to her.

All of them followed in her wake, including her mother. They were assembled behind her like the Atlantic Wall on D-day. And before she could even tell them to back off, there was a firm knock on the front door.

This was going to be a disaster. The worst part was that she actually cared her night was going up in flames. And not in a good way.

Chapter Four

The door opened onto Fiona standing there in a dark green dress, and Brendan could only stare. The material hugged her curvy body and made him ache in places he never knew he had. And the earthy color of it released the fire in her red hair. Not for the first time he thought she was the most beautiful woman he'd ever seen. So beautiful, in fact, that it took him several heartbeats to take his eyes off her long enough to notice the four other people lined up behind her. An older man and woman, probably her parents, and two big strapping men. No doubt the brothers she'd mentioned—Ronan and Keegan.

Right then he felt really stupid in general, but even more so with the single rose in his fingers. Her family was staring at it—and him—as if he was from another planet.

Brendan held the flower out to her and said, "This is for you."

"I figured." She glanced over her shoulder at the lurkers, then met his gaze and rolled her eyes. "Brendan Tanner, these are my parents, Maureen and Paddy O'Reilly. And my older brothers, Ronan and Keegan. Everyone, this is Brendan."

"Tanner," Paddy said as he shook his hand. "So you're the fella who fixed my tractor when I couldn't."

"I've seen the problem before, Mr. O'Reilly. I've worked on a lot of ranches that had tractors, a lot of different models. Including that one. I knew what to look for so it wasn't a big deal."

"I suppose that makes me feel a bit better," the older man said a little grudgingly.

"It was very nice of you to come by and look at it." Maureen O'Reilly was still a beautiful woman and her daughter was her spitting image. "And very neighborly of you not to charge us for your time."

He glanced at Fiona, who wouldn't quite look him in the eyes. So she hadn't told them that his fee had been taking her to dinner. She'd apparently told them he did it as a favor, out of the goodness of his heart. That almost made him laugh, since the jury was out on whether or not he had a heart.

Actually he was glad she hadn't told them the whole truth. He would feel ten times as stupid as he already did. Neighborly wasn't exactly how he felt looking at her in that dress. And the three men staring him down knew it. Could this get any more uncomfortable?

"So, how do you like Rust Creek Falls?" Ronan's tone was friendly enough, but the look in his eyes said, *Hurt my sister and I'm coming for you.*

"It's a nice town." Brendan met his gaze, refusing to look away.

"People around here have each other's backs," Keegan said. "We protect our own. It's how we roll."

"Understood." Brendan met the other man's steely gaze and took some satisfaction when Keegan blinked first.

"Where are your manners, Fiona? We've been talking out here and you should have invited the man in." Maureen looked at her daughter, then back at him. "Would you like to come inside, Mr. Tanner?"

"Mom," Fiona said, "we have a dinner reservation."

Brendan was pretty sure the look she gave him was saying she knew that probably wasn't true but just go with her on it. That worked for him. "We should get on the road. Thanks anyway, Mrs. O'Reilly."

"It's Maureen."

"Yes, ma'am." He looked at Fiona. "You ready?"

"So ready." She slid a black shawl around her shoulders and stepped outside, onto the porch. "'Bye, everyone."

"Nice to meet you all," Brendan said, then settled his hand at the small of her back. The gesture was polite, but also selfish, an excuse to touch her. And it backfired. The contact made him want to pull her close. Suddenly, being polite was the last thing on his mind.

After opening the passenger door, he glanced over his shoulder and saw light still spilling out from the front door, telling him the family continued to watch. Maybe the reminder to mind his manners wasn't such a bad thing, after all. He helped her inside the truck and closed the door. When he walked around the front of the vehicle, he gave the O'Reillys a farewell wave, then got in and headed for the road that would take them out of Rust Creek Falls.

"About that having a reservation remark—" Fiona started. "I was afraid you were going to take my mom up on the invitation to go inside."

"No." He couldn't imagine the seventh level of hell being more uncomfortable than that. "Hope that's okay."

"Very much okay."

"Good." That meant he'd interpreted her look correctly. His instincts in a combat situation had saved lives more than once, but understanding a woman's expression was a thousand times more complex. He often read women's signals wrong but tonight wasn't one of those times.

"Ironically," he said, "I did make a reservation."

"That's good."

"No big deal. I did it online."

"I meant the part where I wasn't actually lying to my mother. That's never good."

"I guess not."

Probably he'd told his mother whoppers but he couldn't remember because he'd been five when she left. And growing up watching his dad be sad without her was pretty bad. No one had ever come right out and said it was Brendan's fault, but he figured a case could be made.

"I'm sorry about that." Fiona's voice broke into his dark thoughts.

For a couple of beats he was afraid he'd spoken out loud, then realized he hadn't. So he was forced to ask, "About what?"

"You specifically said no family. Most of the time mine is scattered. Everyone doing their own thing. Sadly, this wasn't one of those nights. If they made you uncomfortable, I apologize."

"That's not necessary. I'm tough. And they obviously love you."

"I know." She sighed. "But I'm not a teenager and this isn't my first rodeo."

"You're lucky to have them." Said the man who had no one.

"Agreed." She blew out a small breath and looked out the passenger window, but it was too dark to see anything. "So, where are we going?"

"That's a surprise."

"Am I overdressed?"

Yes, he thought, glancing at her in the passenger seat,

then returning his eyes to the road. He would give almost anything to see her without that sexy green dress. But that's not what she meant. And from the online intel he'd gathered, what she had on was perfect for the restaurant. He'd added a navy sport coat to his long-sleeved light blue dress shirt that was tucked into his newest jeans.

"You're fine," he said. "You look really nice, by the way. I should have said so earlier but the welcoming party kind of threw me off my game."

"And I should have thanked you earlier for the rose. But my family circled the wagons and sucked all the oxygen from the air." She let out a sigh. "And you look very handsome."

"Shucks, ma'am—"

She laughed and the sound was like sunshine. It was warm and bright and made him grin. Smiling wasn't natural but there was no holding it back even if he wanted to.

The light moment dissolved his tension and he felt relaxed for the first time in longer than he could remember. Between military deployments and watching his father waste away from cancer, there hadn't been much to smile about. But he'd had a clear understanding of his mission in each case. Sunshine Farm had caught his attention because it was a place where someone could find a fresh start. So far he didn't feel the objective was coming together. So he continued his plan to get back in shape and reenlist.

"It's awfully quiet over there," Fiona said. "Except for the part where I can hear you thinking."

"Oh? How?"

"There's a strange sort of whirring, clunking sound."

"That's just me concentrating on the road." He chuckled again, feeling his connection to her strengthen.

"Hmm," she said thoughtfully. "I could help you watch

the road if I knew where we were going. Although it has to be Kalispell. There aren't many places in Rust Creek Falls that require a reservation."

She was right about their general destination, but he wasn't going to confirm. "Good try, but I'm not going to reveal anything."

About thirty minutes later the lights of the city glowed and twinkled in the distance. From browsing the internet he knew Kalispell was a city of about twenty-two thousand. It was definitely bigger than Rust Creek Falls, which had a nice restaurant at Maverick Manor. He just figured the two of them would draw attention there, which he didn't want. This would be better. Just dinner; no expectations. Always best not to have any.

Enough with the dark thoughts. As best he could, for the rest of the night he was turning them off. It was just a couple of hours. Surely he could manage that.

A short time later he pulled into the restaurant parking lot and turned off the truck engine. "Surprise."

"North Bay Grill. This looks nice. How did you find it?"

"How does anyone find anything these days?"

"Internet," they both said together.

Brendan did a quick scan of the outside and surrounding area. An old habit from deployment days. The wood siding was light blue with white painted shutters bracketing the windows. There were neatly trimmed shrubs and flowers around the perimeter.

"It looks like a New England fishing village." Fiona glanced over at him and smiled.

There it was again. That look as if he'd done just the right thing.

He stared at her for several moments, soaking it in.

Then he forced himself to mobilize and open the door. It was either get moving or kiss her, and he couldn't do that.

"Let's go in," he said.

He went around to the passenger side to open her door but she was already sliding to the ground. Shame. He would have liked an excuse to put his hands at her waist and lift her down. Side by side—he was careful not to touch her—they walked to the entrance and he opened the door for her. It was a weeknight and the place wasn't busy. Apparently a reservation wasn't necessary. The hostess showed them to a table for two by the dual-sided rock fireplace in the center of the room.

Fiona sat down, then looked around at the pictures of ships on the walls and the antique fishing paraphernalia decorating a shelf near the ceiling. "Very cozy on a cold October night."

"Yeah."

A waiter in uniform black pants and a crisp white shirt walked over. "Good evening. My name is Jeremy. I'll be your server tonight. Can I get you something to drink?"

They ordered—chardonnay for Fiona, beer for Brendan—then perused the menu. By the time their drinks arrived, they'd both decided on salmon. Jeremy put a basket of freshly baked cheddar biscuits on the table, then discreetly withdrew. Fiona took one and buttered it before biting.

"Mmm." She closed her eyes and savored the taste.

The look of ecstasy on her face was the sexiest thing he'd ever seen. She looked like a woman who'd been well and thoroughly made love to and he badly wanted to be the man who was responsible for it. The knot in his gut tightened another notch.

Fiona pushed the basket closer to him. "You have to try these."

Anything to take his mind off sex. He snagged one, buttered and bit into it. "Good."

"That's the best you've got? It rocked my world."

Before he could answer, the salads arrived and they both dug in.

Fiona wasn't one of those women who ate two leaves and called it a night. She enjoyed her entire meal and he liked that about her.

"Wow," she said, setting her fork on the empty dinner plate a while later. "I was hungry."

"Me, too." He took a swallow of beer and sat back. "So tell me, have you finished your article?"

She nodded. "I'm working on another one now."

"Already?"

"The extra money is nice." She shrugged.

"What is this one about?"

"Holidays in a small town. 'Tis the season coming up and the best rule is to write what you know." She toyed with the stem of her wineglass. "Halloween isn't far off and next thing you know Thanksgiving will be here. Big cities have their professionally decorated store windows but the people of Rust Creek Falls are every bit as enthusiastic about our traditional ways of celebrating."

"So you're going to write about it."

"Yes. I'll give you a copy and you can let me know what you think."

"I look forward to it."

She glanced at the flames crackling nearby, then back at him. "What do you think about Rust Creek Falls so far?"

"Nice town."

"That's what you told my brother. I was hoping for a couple of details. I guess you're meeting a lot of folks, what with fixing their stuff?" She picked up her glass and took a sip of wine.

"Yes. And being busy is good."

"The fact that you are should tell you something."

"Like?" He watched her settle her hands in her lap.

"There's a real call for what you do. You're providing a necessary service or you'd be twiddling your thumbs."

"Did Luke put you up to that?" he asked.

"What?"

"He said the same thing. I just wondered if he recruited you to talk me into his repair shop whim."

"Maybe it's not just a whim. Maybe he's onto something." She held up her hands to stop him from interrupting. "And no, he didn't enlist my help."

"Okay. Just crossed my mind. He's not shy about sharing his ideas."

"What else is he talking up?"

"We already talked about him doing a little matchmaking."

"Are you saying he's responsible for you asking me to dinner?" Was there an edge to her voice?

Brendan hated to admit it but the man had gotten into his head some. Luke had said he thought Fiona was interested. That thought had been rattling around when he'd fixed O'Reilly's tractor then asked Fiona out to dinner. But no one had held a gun to his head; the words had come out of his own mouth.

"Luke is absolutely not why I asked you to dinner. What he would call this is public relations. Your father will pass on to someone else the positive experience he had with me." He shrugged.

"Publicity through word of mouth," she mused aloud. "A good marketing technique. Especially in Rust Creek Falls."

Brendan ignored the part of his rational mind that suggested Luke's words had fallen on fertile ground and taken root. He wanted to ignore the connection he felt with Fiona. It was happening too fast. It was scary that he felt anything at all. He wanted her bad but that wasn't going to happen. His certainty about it had nothing to do with her not being that kind of girl and everything to do with the fact that he had never felt this way about a woman. He wouldn't let himself go there. He wouldn't end up a sad man, brooding for the rest of his life about the woman who left him.

For Pete's sake, why hadn't he just let Fiona pay him for fixing the damn tractor?

After dinner they left the restaurant and returned to the truck. Fiona climbed into the passenger seat while Brendan held the door for her. The gentlemanly gesture seemed as normal to him as breathing and she found it so darn appealing.

"Thanks," she said.

"You're welcome." His tone was polite but cool all of a sudden.

Why? What had changed now that there wasn't a cloth-covered table between them?

He got in and started the engine. After backing out of the parking space, he headed for the exit and the street beyond that that would take them back to Rust Creek Falls.

In spite of the fact that Luke Stockton seemed to be playing Cupid, she had to admit she'd had a good time. There was no harm in one fun evening out and she wasn't ready for it to end. Fiona wanted to keep it going as long as possible.

She glanced over at Brendan, and in the lights from

the dashboard she could see that his features had settled into what she thought of as brood mode.

Unacceptable.

Since he didn't seem inclined to break the silence, she would. The question was, how? She needed a conversation starter and the idea gods were with her when she came up with something that just might engage him.

"So, that was a nice place," she started.

"Yeah."

"I would definitely recommend it."

"Affirmative."

She wasn't discouraged by the one-word responses. This was leading him right where she wanted to go. "Kalispell is a nice town."

"Yup."

"Okay, look. It's a bit of a drive back and it will be more entertaining if we chat. Don't you think?"

"Sure. About?"

She was ready. "Tell me something about yourself that would surprise me."

Frowning, he glanced over at her, then returned his gaze to the road. "Is that a trick question?"

"Not when it got five words out of you as opposed to one." She was pleased to have his attention. "It's a conversation starter."

"I'm just not sure what you mean by surprise you."

"Well…" She thought for a moment. "I know you were in the Marines and that you're good at fixing things. And tools are your friends. You're a man's man." *Be still my heart*, she thought. "So I'd like to know something about your softer side. Maybe you knit body armor. Use lavender vanilla motor oil. Prefer salad to rare steak. Maybe quiche."

There was a half-smile on his face for a moment before it disappeared. "I left the Marine Corps to help my father when he got sick. The military taught me to fight, but cancer is a battle he and I couldn't win. That's a tough reality for a warrior."

"I can imagine. But I already knew that."

"It was more than that, though. I realized soon enough that the mission changed. I appreciated spending time with him and I nursed him."

"You mean taking him to doctor appointments?"

"That, too. But I handled his meds. Made him as comfortable as possible." There was sadness in his voice. "At the end I fed him when he was too weak to pick up a fork. I made sure his final wishes were attended to."

"He was lucky to have you."

"There wasn't anyone else," he said.

Why? she wanted to ask. What happened that he had to grow up without a mother? It seemed too forward to ask, so she didn't.

"I'm so sorry for your loss. I know that doesn't help, but it's all I've got. I have no frame of reference to understand how you feel except that it must suck to lose a parent. If there's any comfort to be had, it's that he *was* lucky to have you."

"Leon, my dad, said as much, but I'm not sure I believe him. Fathers have to say that."

"Not mine. Paddy O'Reilly doesn't hesitate to say if any of his children are not living up to his high standards." She toyed with the rose he'd given her earlier, which she'd taken with her. "He also would tell you that he loves you unconditionally in front of the whole town at the top of his lungs. The good stuff carries a lot of weight when you know that he won't hold back on the bad."

"I can see how that would be the case." Brendan had

one hand on the steering wheel, easily controlling the truck on the straightaway road.

"So, you never knew your mother?" The words popped out of her mouth and hung in the air between them. She glanced at his profile and noted that he wasn't frowning any more than usual. Neither had he responded to the question.

When he did say something, it was clear he didn't intend to answer. "Your turn. Tell me something about you that would surprise me."

She figured it would take a lot to surprise him and just went with the biggest shock she'd ever gotten. "My boyfriend got a girl pregnant and married her. In that order. I found out at a baby shower. Not for the trollop in Thunder Canyon that he dumped me for. A friend of mine in Rust Creek Falls was having a baby."

Brendan was quiet for a moment then he said, "So, he's not your boyfriend anymore, right?"

That surprised a laugh out of her. The cheating and the public way she'd found out about it had left deep, painful scars. Never in a bazillion years would she have expected to laugh about it.

"No, we are no longer together. He was a stranger in town that I thought I knew. We got close pretty fast and everyone in Rust Creek Falls expected me to flash an engagement ring any second." Surprisingly the painful memory didn't cut as deeply as it once had. "Instead he left. I suppose I should have suspected something when phone calls became infrequent texts that suddenly stopped. But obviously he worked fast and I didn't want to see it, I guess. Then I went to Paige's baby shower and friends from Thunder Canyon who didn't know about my relationship with him shared the 'good' news."

"That falls into the 'really sucks' column."

"You'll get no argument from me." She sighed. "I have more than one regret about the whole awful mess, but the biggest one is that I never got to tell him off."

"Now, that surprises me. You don't strike me as the kind of woman who holds back."

"I'm not. And I thought a lot about what I'd say. Maybe I was waiting for him to do me the courtesy of a phone call to end it." She glanced over at Brendan. "For the record, there are worse things than a breakup text. Radio silence means you were too insignificant to even waste a couple of seconds composing a message."

"And you didn't call him."

It wasn't a question. "I didn't want him to think he was important enough to spend that much emotional energy on."

"I'm pretty sure guys don't contemplate the meaning of emotional energy. If nothing else it would have made you feel better."

"Yeah. But that was a couple years ago and the moment is gone. He's nothing to me now." Except the man her brother Ronan had set her up with. The whole experience was now just a cautionary tale.

He turned onto the road that led to her house. "Almost there. You were right about talking making the time go faster."

"It flies when you're having fun." And reliving painful memories. Her house was just ahead and the front porch light was on.

Brendan parked the truck and turned off the engine, throwing them into darkness. So, here they were, and she'd just bared her soul about the man who'd done her wrong. Now she was facing the "how do you say goodnight?" moment. Hug? Handshake? Kiss on the cheek?

Lip to lip was her preference, but there was no reason to expect that.

She grabbed her purse and the rose in one hand, then opened her door and slid out. Meeting his gaze across the truck's interior, she said, "Thank you for dinner, Brendan. That was very nice of you. I'm sure we'll see each other around. Good night."

She closed the door and headed for the walkway to the porch. Behind her, she heard him get out of the truck, and moments later he fell into step beside her.

"The least I can do is see you safely to your door."

"Don't take this the wrong way, but this isn't a Halloween slasher movie. It's highly unlikely that someone will jump out of the shadows to attack me."

He shrugged. "Call me old-fashioned."

Naturally. And call her a sucker for courtly manners, she thought. A glow started inside her, and she felt sure it was visible from space.

They walked up the steps onto the porch and stopped a few feet from the door. She turned to him and looked up—way up.

"Well, thanks again," she said. "I had a really nice time."

"Me, too."

Was it her imagination that he leaned toward her? She held her breath, and her heart beat so hard it sounded in her ears. Anticipation poured through her.

And then he took a step back. "Good night, Fiona."

In stunned silence she watched him walk away and get in the truck. So, this was a horror movie, after all. But it was her expectations that were slashed. She'd been so sure he was going to kiss her. Until he didn't. And she'd bought a new outfit for this? Some impression she'd made. Apparently he just wasn't that into her.

Never one to miss a chance to see the silver lining,

Fiona rationalized the heck out of this. It was déjà vu. Brendan Tanner was a stranger, a nice hunky one, but they'd been pushed together by a well-meaning man. It was for the best that he didn't kiss her because around him her wisdom and willpower seemed to evaporate. If history was anything to go by, giving in to the attraction would not end well.

But none of that rationalization took away the sting of her bruised ego or the smarting of rejection.

But she'd handled it once. A little chocolate along with reading a couple of sarcastic blogs to shore up her attitude and she would be just fine.

Chapter Five

"We're almost there." Luke glanced over from the driver's side of his truck.

"I was wondering if you were lost," Brendan said.

Luke had asked him to help with roundup this year and they were headed to the cabin to make good on his promise. In October ranchers went into the hills and gathered up cattle that had been grazing there during the summer. Luke had explained that this operation took about three days, and the staging area with cabins, pens for the cows and a stable to put up the horses was a three-hour drive from Rust Creek Falls.

Of course Brendan had been happy to do it. But that was before he found out he'd have too much time to think about Fiona. Too many miles to remember every detail of their dinner the other night, including the fact that he hadn't kissed her good night. He'd wanted to—bad. He was pretty sure letting that opportunity get away from him would be at the top of a long list of regrets.

But on the drive home from Kalispell, because he'd been talking about his father after Fiona had asked him to surprise her, the warning his old man had pounded into him was right there in his head. Brendan still remembered the exact words: *Don't fall in love, son. Don't you dare do it. Then no woman can hurt you like your mother did me.*

Brendan had figured it was pretty important to his dad since the warning was one of the last things Leon said to him before he died. But it wasn't necessary. Brendan had lived the message. His father's wife walked out and later a long-term girlfriend did the same. The experiences hollowed out Leon's heart and made him a two-time loser. Brendan's own growing-up years were all the warning he'd needed, and he swore a long time ago not to let any woman in.

Then he met Fiona O'Reilly.

"You're not very good company," Luke said. "I have better conversations with my horse."

"He's back there." Brendan angled his thumb toward the horse trailer that was hitched to the truck. "I'm happy to switch places with him."

"Now that's what I'm talking about." Luke grinned as he guided the vehicle off the paved road onto a solidly packed dirt one. "I could have used much more of that guy for the last three hours."

"That guy is up for the challenge."

"Too late. We're here." His friend came to a stop beside two trucks already parked in the small compound.

There were two log cabins, side by side, with a couple of wooden picnic tables out front. A short distance away were several empty enclosures that, presumably, would hold the cattle they rounded up. Next to that was a barn—open on both ends—with a roof and stalls to stable the horses. The land was hilly and covered with grass and scrub.

Overhead the sky was a cloudless blue, letting the sunshine take some bite out of the chill in the air. The word *idyllic* came to mind, and it would have been if he hadn't spent the last three hours thinking about a woman he wanted but needed to avoid like the flu.

"Jamie's not here yet. The slacker," Luke teased.

"The man has triplets," Brendan reminded him. "Maybe you should cut him a break."

"I'll give it some thought."

"You might want to decide before those three kids are teenagers."

"Three teens at the same time." Luke shuddered. "I don't know what you were like at sixteen, but I wouldn't wish three of me at that age on my worst enemy. And one of them a girl. You're right. That's when he'll need the slack."

That said, the two of them got out of the truck and looked around. Brendan didn't recognize the other vehicles. "If Jamie's not here, who do those belong to?"

His question was answered when Fiona walked out of the cabin nearest them. A feeling rolled through him that felt like Friday afternoon of a long holiday weekend. Happy to see her didn't do justice to what he felt and he wasn't especially thrilled about that.

When Luke stopped beside him, Brendan said low enough so only his friend could hear, "You didn't mention the O'Reillys would be here."

"No?" Luke shrugged and met his gaze. The expression on his face was just a little too innocent. "The O'Reillys are here. The cattle carry the brands of our respective ranches. Every year we combine our resources to round up the animals and separate them into pens. I hope that's not a problem."

Brendan saw Paddy, Ronan and Keegan come out of the barn and head in his direction. He blew out a long breath. "Not a problem for me."

Then Brendan's gaze zeroed in on Fiona's mouth. *That* was a problem.

"Hello, Luke." Paddy led his brood in handshakes.

"You've all met Brendan, I assume?" Luke's question was met with nods all around. "He's helping us out this year. He has some ranching skills being that he's from Texas. I told him Montana would show him the right way."

Paddy laughed, but his boys didn't react. Apparently glaring at him took all their concentration.

"Good to see you, Tanner."

"How are you, Mr. O'Reilly?"

"Can't complain," the older man said.

Brendan suspected his sons could and would answer differently. He would admit to not always treating women with the respect he should have—promising to call when he had no intention of following through, classic crap that guys pulled—but he hadn't put a disrespectful finger on Fiona. If they were aware of that, it didn't seem to matter.

"How was the drive?" Luke asked the older man.

"Good." Paddy looked up at the perfect sky. "But the weather is due to take a turn. You know how unpredictable October can be in Montana."

"Yeah. I think we're getting this done just in time." Luke nodded. "Jamie's on his way. I planned to give my brother a hard time about always being late but Brendan reminded me he has three kids who will all turn into teenagers at the same time. Figured he needs to save up energy for that."

"Amen." Paddy glanced at his adult children. "It's a load off a father's shoulders when his kids grow up to be fine human beings."

"Thanks, Dad." Fiona smiled at him. "That might be the nicest thing you've ever said to me."

"Don't let it go to your head," he teased her.

"I'm going to take care of my horses," Luke said. "Fiona, would you do me a favor and show Brendan around? Give him the first-timer tour?"

"Sure." The brim of her brown Stetson shadowed her eyes so there was no way to read her reaction to the request. "Grab your gear and I'll show you where to put it."

"Okay." He opened the rear of the four-door truck and took out his duffel, then turned to see she was waiting for him.

His intention was to make eye contact, but damned if his gaze didn't go rogue and land on her lips again. If he'd gone with his instincts that night, he would already know how she tasted instead of letting his thoughts run wild with the unknown. But he hadn't kissed her and was now forced to use his imagination.

"This way." Fiona pointed to the cabin closest to the holding pens.

He fell into step beside her. For some reason he felt the need to break the tense silence. "How've you been?"

"Fine."

He waited for her to take over the conversation and run with it, but that didn't happen. "How's the latest article going?"

"Good."

Zero for two, he thought when she didn't elaborate. Miss Get the Conversation Started didn't seem inclined to want to follow her own advice.

She had surprised him with the story of her bad experience. Brendan was no saint but he would never cheat on a woman and he wanted five minutes alone with the guy who'd done that to her. Even though he had no right to it, anger burned through him, bright and hot.

They stepped on the porch and their boots thudded on the wood. She pushed open the door and led him inside.

"It's basic," she said, "but there's running water and indoor plumbing." She pointed out the open room. "Kitchen, eating area, a couple of bedrooms and bath downstairs. Upstairs are two more bedrooms and a loft. Pick a spot and stash your stuff."

"Okay. I assume your family is in the other cabin?"

"Yes."

This was not the carefree, happy woman he'd had dinner with. He wanted that woman back.

"Are you okay, Fiona?"

"Fine."

Liar, he wanted to say. *Tell me what I did.* But he didn't get a chance to say anything because she turned abruptly and started toward the door.

"We trade off cooking meals for everyone," she said over her shoulder. "Jamie handled it last year so meals will be in our cabin this time."

"Okay. If you need help I can—"

"No." She glanced around, everywhere but at him. "That's it, then. Dinner is at six." And without another word she walked out the door.

Brendan dropped his duffel and followed her. She was headed for the other cabin and he started after her. Before he could catch up, someone behind him called out his name.

It was Ronan. "I need a word, Tanner."

The snarl in the other man's voice said this wasn't going to be a "welcome to the neighborhood" conversation. He turned and faced Fiona's older brother. "What can I do for you, O'Reilly?"

"Why are you here?"

"Like Luke said. To lend a hand."

The other man folded his arms over his chest. "That's it? Just helping out?"

Brendan knew where this was going, but he didn't plan to make it easy. "What other reason would there be?"

"Maybe your motivation has something to do with my sister?"

"I didn't know she would be here. Luke didn't mention that any of you were coming."

All of it was true but Ronan didn't look like he was in the mood to believe that. Brendan wouldn't have agreed to come if he'd known, but it was unlikely this pissed-off older brother would believe that, either.

"So you're here out of the goodness of your heart?"

Luke had asked on Jamie's behalf and Brendan couldn't say no to the man who had given him a place to get a fresh perspective. He considered him a friend who asked for a favor. That was good enough. Did that fall into the "goodness of his heart" category? Close enough. "Yeah. I'm a prince of a guy."

"Then why is Fiona upset?"

"She's your sister. How am I supposed to know?"

Ronan's gaze narrowed on him. "She was fine until you took her out to dinner. She was cheerful, happy, taking care of everyone like always. She was just…Fiona."

"And what? She turned into someone else?" Brendan couldn't resist needling this guy, but he braced himself. No telling how hotheaded he was.

Ronan's glare intensified. "Don't be an ass."

"Too late."

"On the drive up here she was good. When you showed up she wasn't. I don't know. Her mood changed."

"I have no idea what's going on with her. Maybe you should try asking her about this."

"I will." The conviction in his tone said he would do just that. "And one more thing."

"There always is." Brendan barely held back his annoyance.

"I saw the way you looked at her."

"And how was that?" Again with the knee-jerk comment. Brendan knew *exactly* how he'd looked at her.

"I think you can figure that one out for yourself." If possible, Ronan's expression turned even hotter. "Fair warning. If you hurt my sister—"

"Before you finish that thought, you should know I'm an ex-marine. I have advanced hand-to-hand combat training."

"All the same…you've been warned. No one hurts her again."

He walked away before Brendan could respond. He was aware that big brothers could be protective, but this man had a level of hostility that took it up a notch. And the best explanation was that Ronan felt he was somehow to blame for her being hurt. Why?

Brendan meant what he'd said. He wouldn't do anything to make Fiona unhappy and the best way to avoid that was to keep his distance. But damn it. Being warned off made him want her even more.

Of all the roundups in all the world, Brendan Tanner had walked into hers. *How is that even fair?* Fiona thought. At dinner she'd managed to avoid him, and everyone turned in early to rest up for a long day in the saddle. She'd tossed and turned all night and was now in said saddle and feeling tired and pretty doggone crabby about the whole situation.

She and Ronan had paired off and were riding in the hills. From previous years they knew the cows wandered off a fair distance and it was best to start there, then head back to the staging area with as many animals as they could find. The strategy avoided having to double back while keeping the strays together.

It was a Montana Visitors Bureau kind of day. Blue sky dotted with puffy white clouds. The air smelled of earth and shrubs and early morning dew. She loved riding and taking in the beauty of the great outdoors. All these sensations were going into a journal for an article she was planning to write about the experience.

Normally she loved roundup, but this time she wasn't feeling it. Normally she made an effort to chat up whoever she was riding with, but she wasn't feeling that, either. After all, this was Ronan, and her brother didn't care whether or not she kept him entertained with witty conversation. Although he kept giving her funny looks.

"What?" she finally said.

"Excuse me?"

"You keep staring at me. Why?" she snapped.

"I know you're going to bite my head off for saying this, but—" he blew out a breath "—is it that time of the month?"

"Are you seriously asking me that?"

"It's a legitimate question," he defended.

Fiona noted that he looked a little skittish and took some satisfaction from that. Her big, badass, chick-magnet brother might just be a little afraid of her. For however long it lasted she had the power and would abuse it to the best of her ability. And, yes, she realized her pique was directed at someone else and Ronan was in the wrong place at the wrong time. Tough noogies.

"Define a legitimate question," she said.

He squirmed in the saddle as the horses walked side by side. "It's just that you're usually so perky. Asking about everyone else and—"

"Are you saying I'm not pulling my weight this year?

Because that's just baloney. I've fetched, carried, cooked and done my fair share of the chores."

"That's not what I meant."

"It sounded like that's what you meant. So explain it to me." She gave him a look that would have lasered paint off the side of a barn. "For once try talking about your feelings."

"Okay." There was irritation in that one word. "I'm *feeling* that you're not yourself. That you're ticked off about something and not especially cheerful or fun to be around."

"Excuse me. I didn't realize that amusing you was part of getting the job done."

"Not fair, Fiona. There's a burr under your saddle and you're taking it out on me."

Guilty, she thought. He was more emotionally aware than she'd given him credit for. "There are other reasons for a woman's bad attitude besides it being that time of the month."

"So I'll take that as a no on the monthly thing." He met her gaze and she confirmed with a nod. "At the risk of pissing you off more, it's a little early to be wearing the Halloween witch costume."

She really couldn't argue with that characterization. "I'm just having a bad day."

"That's not like you," he commented. "Usually you're so cheerful and optimistic it makes my teeth hurt."

"Then your teeth should be thanking me," she snapped.

"See, that's what I'm talking about. That was a sarcastic comment. Usually those same words would have been teasing."

"Are you saying you don't like my tone?"

"Yeah, pretty much."

"I say again—tough."

"Come on, Fee, I'm your big brother. You can talk to me about anything. We established it's not that time of the month so—" He suddenly stopped talking and his gaze snapped to hers. "Are you late? Does that mean you're pregnant? I'm there for you. You have to know that. It will be okay—"

"Take a breath, for Pete's sake. I'm not pregnant."

One had to have sex for that to happen and she hadn't for a long time. That thought brought back the humiliation of Brendan not kissing her. She would have been putty in his hands but he didn't want her at all. Unexpected tears gathered in her eyes and she looked away. The last thing she wanted was for Ronan to see her cry.

"You have a vivid imagination. Maybe you should be the writer," she said.

"I'm not an idiot. And don't tell me that's open to debate," he warned. "Something's up. Why won't you tell me what's going on?"

It was a valid question. She was close to her sisters and discussed everything with them. But since Brenna and Fallon had fallen in love and set up housekeeping with their respective men, Fiona had grown closer to Ronan. He was there on the ranch. Living in the converted barn, but just a short walk from the house. And he took his responsibilities as big brother very seriously.

She didn't really want to talk about it. There was nothing anyone could do. Rejection was her issue to work through and put behind her. But still. Although he hid it pretty well, her brother was a good guy with a soft heart. He didn't deserve this from her.

"You know," he said, "your mood was just fine until Tanner showed up yesterday. Does he have anything to do with your foul temper?" His voice was barely audible over the *clip clop* of their horses' hooves, but intensity wrapped around every single syllable of those words.

"It's not what you think," she said.

"What do you think I think?"

"That he got out of line when he took me to dinner the other night."

"Did he?" Ronan looked at her, his eyes narrowed dangerously.

She laughed, but that was about irony, not amusement. "Actually, it was just the opposite. He couldn't get away from me fast enough."

"So there was no chemistry between you." He sounded both relieved and pleased.

That's just it, Fiona thought. She was pretty sure there were buckets of chemistry and not just from her. When he touched her it was electric. The looks he gave her sizzled. He'd asked her to dinner, and why would he if not for some feeling on his part? If her man radar was that far off, she would give up her matching black lace bra and panties.

"If you must know, he didn't kiss me good night."

"All right, then." There was a high five all over that statement. Then he looked at her face. "Oh. You wanted him to."

If she wasn't on a horse, Fiona believed there was a very real possibility that she'd have cheerfully choked him just then. "Give the man a prize."

"So, he hurt you. Damn it." His horse danced sideways, probably sensing his anger. "Well, you can be sure he won't do it again."

It took several beats before the words sank in, but when they did Fiona's stomach knotted with dread. "How can you be so sure about that? Now that I think about it, you were talking to him yesterday and neither of you looked like it was a friendly chat about the weather. What did you say to him?"

Ronan shrugged. "Doesn't really matter. You're obviously not going to give him another chance."

"Seriously? You can read my mind?" What if Brendan wanted a second chance? That was unlikely, but what if? Did Ronan scare him off? It would be good to know the context of that tense conversation. "What did you say to him, Ronan?"

"I warned him not to hurt you."

Too late. "Why on earth would you do that?"

"Because he's a drifter. Just like the one who broke your heart."

"Oh, Ronan—"

"What? Do not tell me I should have stayed out of it. What kind of big brother would I be if I didn't look out for my little sister?"

He meant well, but that didn't stop her irritation from bubbling to the surface. "While I appreciate your honorable intentions, I'm a big girl. I can take care of myself, thank you very much."

"Because you did such a good job of that?" Ronan said. As soon as the words were out of his mouth it looked as if he'd give almost anything to have them back.

"You fixed me up with that jerk," she shot back.

"I introduced you," he defended. "I met him at Ace in the Hole and thought he was a good guy. Obviously I was mistaken. You will never know how sorry I am about that. I feel terrible about what happened."

And suddenly she got it. The acute overprotectiveness. "You got in Brendan's face because you're trying to make it up to me."

"Maybe."

"Look, it's very sweet of you to be concerned and I

love you for it. But that bad choice and any I might make in the future are mine alone."

"Are you telling me to stay out of your love life?"

"I—" There wasn't anything to stay out of, but this was a stand for her independence. She'd made it an issue and he deserved an answer to the question. "Yes."

"I can't promise you that." He held up a hand to stop her words. "I can tell you that I'll give anyone who comes calling the benefit of the doubt, but if there's anything I don't like, I'm sticking my nose in. If you don't like it—tough."

"Fair enough. Just give me room to make my choice."

There wouldn't be any reason to interfere in her love life because she was never going to be stupid again. Her head was on straight now. Brendan Tanner *was* a drifter and falling for him would be a check mark in the "stupid" column. She was many things, but stupid wasn't one of them.

Chapter Six

"Good chili." Brendan had no idea who made it but he put the words out there anyway because that was the truth. At six he had joined Jamie and Luke Stockton in the O'Reilly cabin around a wooden picnic-style table where meals were being served.

"Glad you like it," Ronan said. "It's my world famous recipe."

His brother snorted. "You never make it the same way twice. *Recipe* is a stretch."

"Keegan, you wouldn't know a recipe if it came up and kissed you on the mouth." Ronan elbowed his younger brother.

"You're not foolin' anyone," his father said. "Throwing beans, meat and seasoning into a pot is the best you can do to get a meal together since our Fiona's ultimatum."

"Which was?" Luke asked.

"She refused to do all the cooking for roundup just because she was the only woman," Paddy explained. "So the boys and I agreed to each be responsible for one evening meal."

"Heaven help us when it's Keegan's turn," Ronan teased.

"I barbecue a mean steak," his brother shot back.

"The corn bread is good, too," Brendan continued. "Practically melts in your mouth."

"Now, that was Fiona's doing," Paddy said proudly. "She's a good cook. Her mother taught her everything."

"I'll never be as good as Mom," she said.

"I don't know about that," Jamie offered. "That macaroni and cheese you make is enough to make a grown man cry. And it's stopped my triplets from shedding tears a time or two."

"Isn't that the truth," Paddy agreed.

She smiled at her father, who was next to her. The "boys" were sitting across from them. Jamie was on her left with Luke on the other side of the table from him. Brendan was on the end, odd man out. There to lend a hand with rounding up the cows but not really a part of this tight-knit group.

That was just a fact. But what he found truly aggravating was that since giving him the two-cent tour, Fiona had gone out of her way to ignore him. And after a long day in the saddle he was tired and hungry—but not for food. He'd been looking forward to seeing *her*. Now she wouldn't even look at him.

The good-natured banter continued between the O'Reilly brothers, who pulled siblings Luke and Jamie into the joking. Without a word, Fiona stood and stepped over the bench before grabbing her plate and eating utensils. She took them to the sink and washed everything by hand, then put them in a dish drainer on the counter. Brendan decided to do the same and joined her there.

"So, I'll just clean up after myself."

"Knock yourself out." She moved away, then grabbed her jacket from a peg on the wall.

Quietly she let herself out the door. The men were still talking and laughing. They didn't seem to notice she'd left, and Brendan figured he sure wouldn't be missed. He set his washed dishes with hers, grabbed a jacket and slipped outside, too.

It was a chilly night but there was a full moon that bathed the landscape in silvery light. He could see Fiona in the distance and followed her. A couple times he lost her along the winding trail, or trees and bushes blocked his line of sight. But he kept on and heard the sound of gurgling water, which was a clue to her final destination.

Moments later he emerged from the trees and saw a clearing by a stream. Fiona was sitting on a fallen tree trunk facing it. Moonlight turned her red hair into a bright beacon, leading him straight to her. If this was a combat situation, his warrior sense would be warning him to stand fast. Danger ahead. Now that he was a civilian, he called it his better judgment and that was telling him to walk away. Turn around and don't look back. But he ignored it.

"Hi." His boots made noise on the rocky river bank and she'd no doubt heard his approach, but he wanted to make sure he didn't scare her. "It's just me."

She glanced over her shoulder, then turned her gaze back to the stream. "Thought you'd be hanging out with the menfolk. Telling off-color jokes."

"No." So, she still wouldn't look at him. "Is that why you came out here? To give them space?"

"I just wanted some fresh air."

"You didn't get enough of that rounding up cows today?"

Instead of smiling, her mouth pulled tight. "I was with Ronan. It was air, all right, but not what I'd call fresh. He's something."

"Yeah."

"This is a pretty spot."

So, they were changing the subject. "It is. Mind if I join you?"

That got her to look up at him and there was surprise in her eyes. Then she shrugged and said, "Suit yourself."

It was the same tone she'd used with her "knock yourself out" comment. As if his presence made no difference to her one way or the other. That rankled and he decided it suited him to sit next to her. So he did.

His shoulder brushed hers and he'd swear there were sparks spiraling in the crisp night air. That would explain why his brain shorted out for a couple of seconds. When he could manage a coherent thought, the best he could come up with was, "There are wild animals out here. Probably best not to be alone."

"Is that why you're here? To wrestle mountain lions who get any ideas?"

There it was. Her teasing humor and biting wit. He'd missed them more than he'd realized. "I have a certain skill set."

"Apparently the male protective streak is strong here in Montana," she said wryly.

"I didn't notice."

"Oh, please. I know Ronan got in your face yesterday. I saw you talking to him. And I know my brother. He was doing that thing he does. Some older brother/younger sister code he feels obligated to uphold."

"It was nothing I can't handle."

"Still, if he made you uncomfortable, I apologize."

"No need." Because he wanted so badly to take her in his arms, Brendan rested his elbows on his knees and clasped his hands together between them. "I would do the same thing if I had a sister as pretty as you."

"Hmm. I don't know whether to say thank you or you need your eyes checked."

"I'd suggest going with the first one. I don't say things I don't mean."

"That's refreshing." There was a trace of sarcasm in her tone.

"It's the truth," he said quietly.

"I wasn't implying that you are in the habit of telling falsehoods—" She sighed. "The thing is, a little context might explain my skepticism and help you understand why Ronan acted the way he did."

"I'm a guy. I get it."

"It's more than just macho swagger. Remember I told you about the guy who I thought was going to propose?"

"And got a girl pregnant?"

"That's the one," she confirmed. "Ronan introduced me to him."

"He fixed you up?"

"Yeah. They met at Ace in the Hole. My brother liked him and he set up a meet."

"Mr. Matchmaker," he commented, trying to reconcile the cupid image in his mind with the Ronan he'd met.

"If you say that to his face…duck." Her smile came and went in a heartbeat. "The thing is, the jerk told me he had to go back to Thunder Canyon for a while. Some things to take care of."

"That's one way to put it."

"I know, right?" She stared at the gurgling water, moonlight reflecting off the ripples. Her delicate jaw clenched, hinting at the anger and hurt she still felt. "He asked me to wait. Promised he would come back to me. Idiot that I am, I believed him. So I waited."

He remembered her saying that communication between them was sporadic before it stopped. "And he didn't have the guts to tell you himself that he's a cheating bastard."

"Yeah. So Ronan feels lower than pond scum and has gone into protective, "touch my sister and die" mode. I'm sorry he confronted you when there's not even anything going on between us."

"If there was," he said, "I would never string you along. I'd never break a promise like that. When I joined the Marines, I took an oath to protect the Constitution of the United States. I still feel the weight and commitment of that vow in a lot of ways, but especially my personal behavior. I don't make promises I don't intend to keep."

"You're a good man, Brendan Tanner. I appreciate knowing that. Even though we're not a thing," she added.

"You're sure about that? Us not being a thing?"

"If we were, you would have kissed me after we had dinner the other night." There was regret in her voice.

That was something he knew all too well. Remorse for things he'd done and things he hadn't. Just yesterday he'd kicked himself six ways to sundown for not kissing her when he'd had the chance. To miss another opportunity would just be wrong. Because Fiona by moonlight tempted him to his limit.

The conflict raged inside him and he didn't make a conscious decision, but he must have instinctively moved toward her. She met him halfway and the next thing he knew, they were kissing. For just a second he was afraid the pressure of her lips was only his imagination, but it was so much hotter that he knew this was real. Even better, he finally knew the texture and taste of her lips—soft as clouds, sweet as candy.

Just like that he was on fire and wanted more. He took her in his arms and pulled her into his lap, where she snuggled against his chest. Their jackets were in the way but he tightened his hold anyway. She slid her fingers into the hair at the nape of his neck and his whole body went hot and hard.

His heart was pounding and he couldn't get enough air into his lungs. He felt like a man drowning, a man sinking into the feel of Fiona, the scent of her skin, the need to touch her everywhere. Her breathless little moans drove him completely crazy and he wanted her here and now.

Then, through a haze of lust, he heard a nearby twig crack, loud as a gunshot in the quiet night. Whether it was an animal or a man, it was enough to break the spell.

He pulled his mouth from hers. "Fiona—"

"What?" She pressed her kiss-swollen lips together and blinked up at him.

"I need to get you back to the cabin before both your brothers and your father come looking."

"Oh. I guess you're right." Reluctantly she pushed herself out of his arms and stood in front of him. "Okay."

Side by side they walked the path back. Neither of them spoke and the air between them crackled with tension. Thoughts tumbled through his mind like rocks rolling down a hill. According to her reasoning, a kiss made them a thing. But he told her he would never promise her something he couldn't deliver.

As badly as he wanted to kiss her and have her in his bed, he could never do that. Fiona wasn't a fling kind of woman, but a fling was all he could give her. It was inevitable he'd let her down. He'd told the truth about not breaking vows and he wouldn't break the one he'd made to himself about never hurting her.

After three and a half awkward days, one of which included the best kiss she'd ever had, Fiona was relieved that it was finally time to pack up and go home. Luke, Ronan and Keegan were driving the cattle back to the ranches.

They were at the barn saddling horses and making sure everything was stowed away and organized for next year. Jamie and Brendan would take two trucks while she rode with her dad. She wanted to brainstorm some ideas for ranching articles with him. Anything to keep from thinking about the way Brendan had distanced himself after that excruciatingly romantic kiss in the moonlight.

At dinner in Kalispell they'd had a great time, and then he skipped the good-night kiss. When he finally did kiss her, she was ready to go wherever he would take her. Which, apparently, was nowhere, based on the fact that he'd barely said two words to her since. That night by the stream it felt to her as if he couldn't help himself, but afterward he resisted her just fine.

She was getting so many mixed signals, this "thing" was giving her whiplash.

"I'm done thinking about him."

And now she was talking to herself as she shoved the last of her clothes into a duffel, then carried it downstairs and out to the truck. She tossed it into the back seat and slammed the rear passenger door.

Her gaze was drawn to the horse trailer hitched to Luke's truck, where Brendan was sweet-talking one of the animals inside. Her heart did a little flip that made a liar out of her. She couldn't seem to stop thinking about him.

If only he wasn't so gosh-darn good-looking. Even as she thought that, she knew it wasn't just about him being handsome. If he wasn't a decent man, Luke and Eva wouldn't have him at Sunshine Farm.

"Something wrong, Fee?"

"Hmm?" She glanced around as her father walked up behind her. "I'm sorry, what?"

"Looked like you were a million miles away." Paddy

put a box of supplies in the bed of the truck, then met her gaze. "Something on your mind?"

"Always. You know me," she said vaguely.

"I do. Better than you think." There was a curious intensity in his eyes. "And I suspect what you're thinking has something to do with the new fella."

She flicked a glance in Brendan's direction. Now he was leaning against the horse trailer, patiently waiting to head out after loading the animals. Looking as if he didn't have a care in the world. What would it take to shake that casual attitude?

"Why would you say that?" she asked her dad.

"There it is." Her father nodded knowingly.

"What?"

"The tone. The one telling me I'm just a man and couldn't possibly understand women. Your mother uses it on me all the time."

"And you always tell her she's right."

"Mostly she is. And she likes hearing it." He grinned, showing a hint of the charmer who'd captured her mother's heart. "But don't you believe that I'm completely clueless about this sort of thing."

Paddy O'Reilly had pretty much let her mom deal with it. Even when Fiona had been the talk of Rust Creek Falls after being dumped, her dad had only muttered that he never liked the rat bastard scum-sucking loser. But he'd never actually talked to her about it. So she was curious about his interest now.

"Define 'this sort of thing,'" she told him.

"Let's just say it didn't escape my notice that you and Tanner disappeared the other night. Together. Just the two of you."

Fiona felt heat creep into her cheeks. She'd hoped no one had noticed that. When not a word was said about it, she'd believed she was home free. "It's not what you think, Dad."

"So you know what I'm thinking?"

She didn't want to spell that out. Not to her father. "We talked. And there is no 'this sort of thing.'"

"If you say so."

"I do."

Paddy didn't respond. He just stared at her. Fiona felt like a little girl again, the one who always cracked and confessed wrongdoing under the pressure of that look. It hadn't seemed like it at the time, but life was easier when she'd been a child. Now she wasn't her father's little girl anymore. She was a grown woman and didn't have to tell him that Brendan had kissed her. And that she liked it. That kiss had rocked her world like an earthquake, but obviously she was the only one feeling aftershocks. Hence, there was nothing between them.

Paddy finally sighed and shook his head. "You're as pretty as your mother and as stubborn as me. I'm not sure that's a good thing, Fiona."

How about that? She'd stared down the master and he got nothing out of her. It was just a small thing, but she still felt proud. "I love you, too, Dad."

"Love is both a blessing and a curse." He fished the truck keys out of his jeans pocket. "I need to start her up and make sure this old girl will get us home."

Seeing Brendan here at the roundup staging area had pushed everything else from her mind. Fiona had forgotten that when they left home, the truck had been running rough. Like all the ranch equipment, her father took care of maintaining his vehicles.

"Are you worried about it?" she asked.

"No. But if there's a problem, I want to know about it before everyone takes off from here." He nodded in Brendan's direction. "Want to make sure I don't need his help. I'll take a look at everything, then start her up."

He walked to the front of the truck and lifted the hood, then leaned in to inspect the engine guts. A couple minutes later he straightened and got in behind the wheel to start it up. Suddenly there was a loud, explosive sound as the engine backfired.

Fiona happened to be looking at Brendan, who instantly dropped to the ground as if he'd been shot. She'd seen enough movies and TV shows and read articles about the challenges of combat soldiers returning to civilian life. Not all the wounds showed on the outside. She didn't have to be a shrink to realize the unexpected boom must have triggered memories of a dangerous war zone, where an explosion meant injury and death.

Almost as quickly as he'd gone down, Brendan was back on his feet. His back was to her so he wasn't aware that she'd seen.

"Doggone it." Her father slid out from behind the wheel and poked his head back under the hood. "That's never good. It could be the spark plugs or a dirty air filter. Or something else."

"Should I get Brendan to have a look?"

"Couldn't hurt," he said. "He fixed the tractor when I couldn't see squat wrong with it. The man is a genius with this stuff."

"Should I tell him you said that?" she teased.

Paddy looked up from the wires and gizmos under the hood. "Can if you want to. Doesn't mean I'm not still watching him real close."

"Don't think I don't appreciate that."

He grinned. "The heck you do. But fathers watch out for their baby girls. Before you say it, I know you're not a baby anymore. Doesn't make a damn bit of difference."

Now that she thought about it, Paddy didn't involve himself in her love life, except to say he didn't like the loser who dumped her. And he was the only one in the family who'd felt that way. What had he seen that no one else had?

"What do you think of Tanner, Dad?"

"Don't have enough information yet to answer that. I can tell you one thing. Serving this country in the Marine Corps goes a long way with me." He straightened and met her gaze. "But you're asking if I like him for you."

"No. It's not like that." Because Brendan had made it clear he wasn't for her. There was no "them." "I was just wondering what you thought."

Her father glanced at the other truck and horse trailer, where the man in question was waiting, then back at her. "It's a long ride home and there will be plenty of time to share my thoughts on everything. But if you don't get on over and ask that fella to have a look at this truck pretty quick, we may never get started."

"Yes, sir."

She headed over to Brendan. The front of him was still a little dusty from dropping to the ground and he was absently brushing it away.

"Hi," she said.

"Hey." He didn't look up.

"Are you all right?" she asked.

"Horses and gear are all loaded up. Just waiting on the others to say the word that we're ready to move out."

Fiona didn't miss the fact that he'd deliberately made her question impersonal. She could play along and pretend she hadn't seen how the truck backfiring had affected him. The others were busy, so no one but her knew how he'd reacted. Or she could ask straight out. A case could be made for either course of action, but the reality was that she just couldn't ignore he was going through something.

"So, the truck backfire was loud," she started.

He looked at her then, and there was a mix of emotions in his clear green eyes. Suspicion. Wariness. Embarrassment that someone had seen. A little residual fear, maybe.

"Could be the catalytic converter," he said.

"Actually, I wasn't asking why. It was more about what happened when you heard it."

His mouth pulled tight for a moment before he shrugged. "I jumped."

"I jumped. You hit the deck, Brendan."

"You saw that, huh?" He looked away for a moment. "Wasn't expecting it."

"Do you want to talk about it?"

"Nothing to say." He slid his fingertips into the pockets of his worn jeans.

"I don't think that's true. You might not want to discuss it but I bet there's quite a bit to fill a conversation. And I'm happy to listen. In fact, Dad doesn't need me. I could ride along with you—"

"As you've pointed out, I'm not much of a talker. Just the way I'm wired, I guess."

"You're not alone," she said. "I've got brothers and they keep things bottled up pretty tight. Probably a guy thing. So I get it."

"Nothing really to get." He lifted a shoulder. "Not much to say."

"Okay. I won't push."

"Good."

"I just have one more thing to say," she told him.

"Why doesn't that surprise me?"

"Maybe because *I'm* wired that way." She stuffed her cold hands into the pockets of her sheepskin jacket. "The other night you told me you don't ever take for granted your oath to protect and defend the Constitution of this country. I'm pretty sure you can't forget things that happened to you in the service of it."

"Fiona, don't make a big deal out of this—"

"I'm almost finished." She heard the beginning of irritation in his voice and didn't care. There was nothing to lose by giving him a piece of her mind. "You don't have to tell me anything. But it might help you to talk to someone." She stopped and looked at him. "Now I'm done."

"Okay. I'm going to see what's keeping the guys." He half turned toward the barn.

"Wait. One more thing."

"What?"

"Dad wanted me to ask you to look at the truck. Make sure you don't see something that can't wait until we get home."

"Okay." He didn't say it, but everything about his body language said he was relieved that she'd changed the subject.

Fiona's heart broke a little bit for him. Everyone needed help sometimes, someone to listen. Even strong men like Brendan Tanner. Clearly he wasn't about to confide in her, but she would really like it if he did.

She would like that way too much.

Chapter Seven

Several days after returning to Rust Creek Falls, Brendan still couldn't forget the way Fiona looked at him. With pity. It made him so mad. Not that he blamed her. She had a soft heart and wanted to help. He was ticked off at himself for not being able to control his reaction to that truck backfiring at the cabin. The unexpected sound had put him right smack in the middle of a firefight in Afghanistan.

Fiona was the last person he would pick to see him like that. He didn't want anyone to feel sorry for him, but especially not her. It was pointless to puzzle out the why of that because A, he didn't do commitment and he wouldn't do anything less than that with her, and B, he was getting into shape to reenlist in the Marine Corps.

It was early afternoon when he pulled his truck to a stop at the curb of a cute little house on South Broomtail Way in Rust Creek Falls. An American flag was proudly displayed in front. Eddie Halstead had asked for his help with a couple of projects. On top of the fact that her husband was a former marine, Brendan wasn't much enjoying his own company right now and figured it couldn't hurt to give them a hand.

The siding on their home was painted green, a shade that reminded him of his woodland utilities uniform. Shutters framing the windows were white. A sidewalk led to three steps and a covered porch. The grass was cut and neatly edged, bushes and flowers strategically arranged. The property was buttoned down, he thought. It definitely passed inspection.

He exited the truck and retrieved his portable tool-box from the back, then headed up the walkway. Moving closer, he saw a sign above the door that said, *"Semper fi." Semper fidelis*—always faithful—the Marine Corps motto.

Brendan felt emotion and pride and something that could have been homesickness all roll into a ball and come to rest on his chest. He missed belonging somewhere, having a purpose, someone else counting on him and him counting on them. Although, now that he thought about it, Eddie was counting on him to do some things around here that she didn't want her husband to do.

He rang the bell and waited. When the door opened, an older man stood there. He was nearly six feet, with silver hair cut military-short and sharp, clear brown eyes. He stood straight, his shoulders back, as if standing inspection.

"You must be Brendan Tanner. The tools are a clue." He glanced at the metal box. "I'm J. T. Halstead."

Brendan shook the hand he held out. "Nice to meet you, sir."

"It's J.T. And just so we're clear, son, it's Eddie's idea for you to be here. I'm perfectly capable of getting on a ladder, but I agreed to please her. Plus, if I fell off and didn't kill myself in the process, she'd never let me live it down."

"Yes, sir." Brendan figured J.T. was a lucky man to

have someone care about him that much. Fiona would care that way.

J.T. shook his head. "I'm still trying to decide whether or not to thank you for fixing that blasted blender. A man drinking his breakfast is just wrong."

"Roger that, sir. Did you sabotage the blender?"

"Wish I'd thought of it," he said wryly.

"Are you going to ask the man in, J.T.?" Eddie's voice was coming from somewhere beyond the doorway. "Hurry up and close the door. I can feel a cold draft all the way back here."

"My bride." There was amusement in the man's expression. "Feel free to salute her. She likes that."

J.T. motioned him inside then shut the door. He turned and started walking toward the back of the house. His gait was uneven, the left leg stiff as the man sort of swung it forward from the hip. The prosthetic leg. This marine had come home from war physically changed yet had figured out how to move on, and Brendan was impressed.

They walked into the kitchen, where Eddie was standing at an island in the center of the room, removing cookies from a pan and setting them on a rack to cool. "Hi, Brendan. Thanks for coming over."

"No problem. Nice place." He looked around the cozy room and breathed in the delicious smell of freshly baked cookies.

On the pale yellow walls there were pictures of parsley, sage, rosemary and thyme. Womanly touches were everywhere, making the room feel like a foreign country to him. Most of his growing-up years had been just him and his dad. Testosterone central.

Then he noticed a couple other wall hangings. One said, "All men are created equal and then a few become brothers. United States Marine Corps." Another read,

"I'm not a hero, but I had the honor of walking beside a few who were." This manly touch made for a nice balance.

Eddie smiled at him and asked, "Would you like a cookie? Maybe a cup of coffee to go with it?"

"Probably I should just get started on that list of yours."

"It's an impressive one," she said, her eyes twinkling. "But when's the last time you had home-baked cookies?"

Brendan wasn't sure he ever had. "Well, if you're sure—"

"You know, Ed, someone should try one—just to make sure they're up to your usual standards." J.T. gave him a wry look. "It's the least a brother can do."

"Oorah." Brendan grinned.

Eddie set two cups of coffee and a plate of cookies on the table along with Halloween napkins. "Here you go."

He sat in one of the ladder-back chairs.

J.T. sat at a right angle to him and automatically kneaded his left thigh, as if it bothered him. But there was no evidence of discomfort in his expression when he smiled at his wife. "Thanks, honey."

"This is my day to call Kyleigh, our daughter who lives in Colorado," she explained to Brendan. "J.T., you're clear on the list?"

"Crystal," he answered.

She met Brendan's gaze. "Do *not* let him step foot on a ladder."

"Understood." He wanted to salute but resisted.

When the two men were alone J.T. said, "That look was the one she used to keep sixth graders in line when their impulse control got out in front of their common sense. She's a retired teacher."

"Could have been a Corps drill instructor," Brendan observed.

"She'd take that as a compliment."

"I meant it as one."

The other man nodded then stirred cream and sugar into his coffee. "So, how long were you in?"

Brendan knew he meant the length of his military service. "Fourteen years. I enlisted after high school."

"You always wanted to be a soldier?"

"Something like that." Mostly he'd wanted to get away from home. He'd signed up before his dad got dumped by yet another woman in his life, then felt guilty leaving Leon alone when he was going through such a rough time.

"How many tours did you do?"

"I deployed to Afghanistan three times."

"Rust Creek Falls is the polar opposite of Kabul," J.T. said.

"Unless a car backfires." Brendan hadn't meant to say that, but he saw agreement in the other man's eyes.

"How long have you been out?"

"Year and a half. My father had cancer. I came home to take care of him." Brendan stared at the coffee in his cup. "He died six months ago."

"Sorry for your loss, son."

"Thank you."

"So you're still adjusting to civilian life."

"*Still* being the operative word. In most ways it feels as if I've just started. The first year with my dad didn't seem to count. It was sort of regimented. Doctors, treatment, drugs, survival."

"And it took your mind off all the things you didn't want to think about."

"Yeah." Something clicked inside him, as if a connection was made and a current of understanding flowed freely. The memories were always there, waiting for something to trigger them. He knew that it had taken the military brass a long time to recognize post-traumatic stress as a very real syndrome for men and women who served in a theater of war.

J.T. obviously lost his leg. He'd come home and all these years later seemed to have a normal life. What had it taken to get him here?

"How did you get past it?" Brendan met the other man's gaze and knew he understood the question. "If you don't mind me asking."

"Not at all." He took a cookie from the plate and bit into it. "We got married before I was drafted and sent overseas near the end of the war. I was lucky enough to have her to come home to. Right away she got pregnant with our first child, Kyleigh. And I didn't have time to think about 'Nam. I had a family to support and I worked as an electrician for a construction company in Kalispell. Days were busy. It was at night when the war terrors came back."

"How so?"

"Nightmares. Things you push away in the day come out then and there's no way to hide it, as much as you'd like to. Eddie's no one's fool."

"What did you do?"

"I was smart enough to open up and talk about what I experienced, and then I let her love the horror of it right out of me."

"Hmm."

"She's the best thing that ever happened to me. And every day I try to let her know it." J.T. drank the last of the coffee in his cup. "Speaking of that, if you're ready, we can start here in the kitchen, replacing that ceiling light. I've got a stepladder in the garage. I'll show you where it is."

For the rest of the afternoon, Brendan chatted with the couple as he went from changing spotlights to putting up outside Halloween decorations to checking out a noise in the refrigerator. But in the back of his mind, the veteran's words rolled around. Love was the answer. If so, that was a problem. What did a marine veteran do when love was the enemy?

Fiona walked into the kitchen and smelled bacon and eggs when her taste buds had been expecting something completely different. "I thought you were going to make Grandma's pumpkin waffles."

"I was." Her mother turned off a burner on the stove. "But Grandma's waffle iron isn't cooperating."

"What's wrong?" Fiona walked over to the counter and lifted the heavy metal lid. "Looks okay to me."

"It won't heat up."

"But it's October. We always have pumpkin waffles on Sundays in October."

"I know." Maureen sighed.

She didn't miss the distress in her mother's eyes that could turn into tears any second. The woman loved her mother's waffle iron. It was one of only a few mementos she had and the thing was used frequently, keeping Grandma's memory alive. Maureen O'Reilly didn't just pull an old appliance out of the cupboard. With it came the stories, tender and quirky, about the feisty woman who had raised her.

"Isn't the batter already made? Can't you make pancakes instead?"

"I could. But the experience isn't the same without the tradition." She sniffled and blinked, stubbornly refusing to give in to tears.

"Maybe Dad can look at it. I'll go get him," Fiona offered.

"No. He already checked it out and pronounced the

thing dead. So he went to mend fences in the north pasture."

"No way. It's family day."

"I got a little emotional."

And her father couldn't stand to see his wife cry, especially if he couldn't make her feel better. "Oh, Mom—"

Maureen shrugged. "He said it was old and maybe it was time to get a new one. But they don't make things like they used to and there's no character in them. Just instructions you can't understand and buttons you don't know what to do with."

"Maybe it can be fixed, Mom."

"I already told you. Your father is ready to throw it out like a used tissue."

"No, I meant Brendan Tanner. He took care of Eddie Halstead's blender. She's singing his praises all over town."

Her mother's expression brightened. "Why didn't I think of that?"

"Because you were upset and there hasn't been anyone in Rust Creek Falls who could do it before. You should take it to him," Fiona suggested.

"That's a great idea." Maureen shook her head. "Would you mind dropping it off for me? I'm making pumpkin bread today. Halloween isn't far off and the holidays will be here before you know it. I have to start the holiday baking and freezing."

Her mother baked a bazillion loaves for gifts and get-togethers from now through Christmas. Maureen O'Reilly's pumpkin bread was a very big deal.

"Don't you need me to help you with that, Mom? The waffle iron can wait. You can drop it off on your way into Rust Creek Falls the next time you go."

Her mother arched one eyebrow. "Is there some reason you're avoiding Brendan?"

"No." Did she say that too fast? "Of course not." Was she protesting too much?

"Then why don't you want to see him?"

Maybe because she wanted too much to see him? If she said that, there would be a talk, which would be a waste of time. He'd kissed her, sampled the wares so to speak, and lost interest. Apparently she didn't light his fire.

"Who says I don't want to see him?" she protested.

"Good. Then take Grandma's waffle iron over to him today. And don't leave until you have a prognosis."

"He's probably not even there, Mom. Since he fixed our tractor, other ranchers have been after him to look at their larger equipment. His skills are in high demand."

"Good. Then just drop it off. You won't have to even see him."

As much as Fiona didn't want to take a chance on seeing Brendan, there was no getting out of this. "Okay."

Maureen O'Reilly wore stubborn like a winter coat. She put it on when necessary, then shrugged out of it when the job was done. She smiled sweetly, then hugged her daughter. "Thank you so much, sweetheart."

So that's why, a few minutes later, with a breakfast sandwich to go, she was on her way to Sunshine Farm with Grandma's on-life-support waffle iron. She couldn't shake the feeling this trip was flirting with fate, but she hadn't done much flirting at all recently. So, what the heck?

After turning off the road onto the property, she smiled. It was hard to look at the sunshine-yellow barn and be grumpy. She parked nearby, then grabbed the square appliance from the seat beside her and got out of the truck. A memory washed over her of chasing little

Jared Stockton into the barn and meeting Brendan Tanner for the first time.

In the looks department he was a standout, but she'd spent some time with him since and found he was so much more than just a pretty face. He had courage, loyalty, integrity—and baggage. Well, who didn't?

She'd really hoped to just leave the appliance and a note because he was out working on someone's tractor, but that turned out not to be necessary. He turned when she walked through the doorway of his workshop.

"Fiona." He sounded a little surprised. "Hi."

Was it her imagination or just wishful thinking that he looked pleased to see her? "Good morning. Although I guess it's almost afternoon now."

"Yeah." His gaze dropped to the appliance she was holding against her chest like armor. "What do you have there?"

She blinked at him, then remembered. Walking closer, she set the thing beside the lamp he was working on. "It's a waffle iron."

"I figured," he said wryly.

"You're probably on your way out to fix something bigger and more important. But when you get a few minutes could you take a look at this? For my mom."

"What's the problem?"

"It won't heat up." She couldn't say the same for her. Standing this close to him made her skin burn. Nonchalance would be so much easier if she didn't have vivid memories of how wonderful it felt to be held in his strong arms.

He lifted the heavy lid and glanced at the individual squares inside. "No heat makes it nothing more than a doorstop." He nodded thoughtfully. "I'll have a look right now."

"I don't want to keep you. But I have explicit orders from my mother to stay until you've fixed the thing or pronounced it dead. But it really can wait."

"I'm in no rush." He laughed. "And this sounds really serious."

Humor transformed his face, making him look younger, more carefree. It was an expression that could have a woman swooning if she wasn't careful. "I don't mean to sound so dramatic, but this means a lot to my mother because it belonged to her mother. She makes waffles and passes on the story of how Grandpa courted Grandma when they were still in high school."

"Sounds special." He was looking at the cord. "This is frayed and that means electrical current isn't getting through."

"Can you fix it?"

"Yes."

"Oh, thank God." She touched a hand to her chest. "My mom will be so relieved."

"Happy to help." He didn't look at her, but his voice took on a wistful note when he asked, "Did you know your grandmother?"

"Yes. She was so wonderful. I miss her, too. She died a couple of years ago, way too young. It's one of the reasons my mom is so sentimental about this thing."

"Hmm."

"What?" She couldn't read his expression.

"I was just wondering what it's like to have a mom," he said.

At dinner the day she'd met him, he made that cryptic remark. *Necessity is the mother I never had.* Fiona had been curious then, but said nothing. She knew him better now and if he didn't want to answer, he would change the subject.

"What happened to your mom?" she asked gently.

"She left my dad when I started kindergarten." He worked while he talked, baring the wires, stripping them with a plier-like tool.

The words and tone were conversational, but devoid of emotion, as if he was talking about someone else. But Fiona's heart hurt for the five-year-old boy he'd been. "She just walked out without a word?"

"No, there were plenty of words. She explained everything to me."

"That must have been one heck of an explanation, because I don't understand how a mother could leave her child."

"She said she'd been unhappy with my dad from the beginning. Turns out she only married Leon because she got pregnant and was scared. She didn't know what to do."

"But you were just a little boy. That's heavy stuff to lay on you."

"There's more."

"Seriously?"

"Oh, yeah." He met her gaze for a moment. "She said she picked the name Brendan because it's Celtic for *sword.* Warriors used swords and I needed to be brave."

"So she never planned to stay."

"Apparently. She waited to leave until I was in school and child care would be easier for my dad. He was handsome and a good man but she needed more excitement. The truth was she wasn't mom material and she said I would be better off with just my dad raising me."

Fiona was stunned at the amount of information the woman had unloaded on such a young child. "I have to say, I agree with her about her lack of maternal instincts."

"You think?"

"I don't know what to say. At least she didn't walk away without a word? Or she's just a selfish witch."

"My dad went with the witch one. And a few other more colorful descriptions that I can't repeat in front of a lady." Mentioning his dad put emotion in his eyes and none of it was the warm and fuzzy kind.

"How did he take it?"

"Nearly broke him," Brendan admitted. "The sadness—" He shook his head. "I was young, but even I could see it."

"I don't remember much from being five," she said. "But I guess a life-altering crisis like your mom leaving is pretty hard to forget."

He inspected the repaired waffle iron cord, then plugged it in to test it. After lifting the lid, he felt the inside and smiled at her. "Heat."

No kidding, Fiona thought. When he looked like that she could almost feel steam coming out of her ears. "My mother will be so happy. She'd give you her first-born, but Ronan might have something to say about that."

"Something tells me you're right," Brendan said wryly. "I'm glad I could help."

"Me, too." Then he looked a little sheepish and she asked, "What?"

"I didn't mean to go on about my past. Don't know why that all came out. Sorry—"

She held up a hand to stop him. "No apology necessary. What are friends for?"

"Is that what we are?"

"I hope so. And friends talk to each other about what's bothering them."

"So, let's even the score. Anything bothering you?"

"Just how much I owe you for fixing the waffle iron."

He thought for a moment. "What about a horseback ride?"

Warning bells were sounding, but she could barely hear because her heart was pounding so hard. "You fix the tractor and buy me dinner, then you repair the waffle iron and want to take me riding."

"Is that a yes or no?"

"It's a 'keep this up and I'll be your best customer.'" She felt as sunny and happy as the cheerful color of this barn. "So, yes, it's a yes."

A big fat affirmative. Because being careful was highly overrated.

Chapter Eight

Brendan wasn't sure about Fiona becoming his best customer, but she was his best *something*. At the roundup he'd looked forward to seeing her every day. When it was over, he'd missed her. When she came in with that waffle iron, he'd been so damn glad to see her. The idea of her just walking away after he'd repaired it made him impulsive. All he could think of to keep her there was a horseback ride.

He'd checked with Luke to make sure borrowing a couple of horses for a ride was all right with him. After being grilled, he had to admit that the second horse was for Fiona. That was all it took for his friend to enthusiastically give the okay. A guy would have to be exceptionally clueless not to get that Luke was all but throwing him and Fiona together. She would probably have a negative opinion after what happened the last time someone fixed her up.

But Brendan couldn't worry about that—or anything else. Not on such a beautiful day. It was cool but sunny. The sky was deep blue and seemed to go on forever. And there was a stunning, sexy woman riding beside him.

As their horses trotted away from Sunshine Farm toward wide-open land, he looked over at her. Her hair gleamed like a brand-new copper penny in the sun. She looked happy and carefree, her body moving with the animal in a graceful, fluid motion. He could stare at her all day, but she'd busted his chops about making conversation, so he racked his brain for a topic.

"I'm sorry your grandmother's waffle iron broke and upset your mother." That was a bald-faced lie. It's what brought her here. "But it's nice to see you."

"Nice to see you, too." The smile she sent in his direction was pleased and a little shy. "And I'm sorry your mom left. You can borrow mine if you want."

"I think she's got enough kids to worry about."

Brendan still wasn't sure why he'd told her about his mother. Might have something to do with his time out at the Halsteads' yesterday. Eddie baked cookies, called her daughter once a week. She was the kind of mother he'd like to have had. And then there was his chat with J.T. The veteran was the second person who'd advised him to talk about the experiences that he couldn't quite forget. Fiona had been the first.

"My mom would never shut anyone out from under her worry umbrella," Fiona said. "If someone needs to be worried about, she's more than happy to oblige."

A maternal quality his own mother had been missing. He glanced over and found Fiona looking back. A feeling crept over him that she was a lot like her mom in caring for people. The way she'd come to him after the truck backfired, quietly checking to make sure he was okay. The answer to that was yes and no. He'd had a combat flashback, but guys he'd served with had it a lot worse. He wished there was something he could do to help get them past the worst like Luke was doing for him.

"You should probably check with your mom before

offering her services to strangers." He was kidding, but her mouth pulled tight for a moment.

"I don't have to check. She's a natural born worrier. If she doesn't have something to fret about, she'll find something. Look at it this way—you'd be doing her a favor."

He laughed. Humor swelled inside him and lit up all the places that had been so dark for so long. He defied anyone to spend time around this woman and not smile. It was healing. Exactly what he'd hoped for when he'd heard about a ranch in Rust Creek Falls that offered a place to stay for someone looking to make a fresh start. Luke's invitation was making it possible for Brendan to take back the life he'd had before his father got sick.

"If I need to be worried about, I'll let her know," he promised.

"I would hope you'd let me know first," she said.

"Sure."

"Really?" She didn't look convinced.

His response had come automatically and he wondered now if it really was true. She'd given him an opening to talk about his battle baggage, but he'd brushed her off. Partly because he didn't want the hell of war to touch her in any way and partly because only someone who'd been through it could understand.

"I've been taking care of myself for a long time," he finally said. "As a soldier it's my job to take care of other people."

"But you're not a soldier now," she said quietly.

"Right." It was hard to shake the military mind-set when that was the only place he'd ever felt he belonged. "I guess fixing things for folks is still taking care of them."

"Can't argue with that. Not only is my mother over the moon that you fixed Grandma's waffle iron, the whole family will reap the rewards of a pumpkin spice waffle breakfast tomorrow. Ranchers around here are ecstatic about your skills with fixing tractors and backhoes. Rumor has it that there's a waiting list for your services. You have so taken care of us."

"Understood." That made him feel good, and Brendan wondered if his father had ever been able to find that perspective about the service he'd provided.

They were quiet for a while as their horses plodded along a crude trail carved through prairie grass. In the distance mountains stood tall and rugged. Straight ahead, just beyond a line of trees, he spotted a stream.

He pointed to it. "That's a good place to rest and water the horses."

"Okay."

Closer to the river bank they stopped, dismounted, then led the animals to the water. When they'd finished drinking, Brendan drew them to nearby grass and secured the reins to a sturdy bush before joining Fiona, who was leaning against the trunk of a ponderosa pine tree.

He stopped beside her and breathed in the clean air— no desert dust, fear sweat or smell of gunpowder anywhere. Peace was taken for granted by anyone who'd never been to war, and Brendan savored this moment, memorizing everything about it. He studied the mountains that seemed closer and bigger from here than they were from Sunshine Farm.

Fiona followed his gaze. "I hear Texas is flat."

"A lot of it is. But there are some mountains in the western part of the state. Somehow this is different."

"In a good way?"

"Yeah."

"Won't be long until there's snow on them," she commented, nodding toward the towering peaks.

For some reason the words made him feel empty and

he was filled with longing. To be in the same place from season to season, year after year. Long enough to know when the leaves would change and the snow would come.

"I look forward to seeing snow. Maybe for the holidays. I've never had a white Christmas."

"Really?" When she looked at him, her eyes sparkled with happiness. "I wasn't sure you would be staying that long."

"The truth is that I haven't figured out my future yet. I can't make you any promises."

"I never asked for one." Her eyes were flashing now but not with anything good. "What makes you think I want a commitment?"

"All I said was it would be nice to see snow. I honestly have no idea what I'm doing tomorrow, so—"

"I'm not saying you have to decide. I made an innocent comment and you pushed back as if I suggested we elope next Sunday. I'm a big girl, Brendan—"

"Yeah. I noticed." Things would be less complicated if he hadn't.

She pushed away from the tree and faced him, standing just inches from him. This was not a good time to finally figure out what it meant that a woman was beautiful when she was angry. And Fiona was more beautiful than he'd ever seen her.

"I can handle the truth, Tanner. Stop sending mixed signals. You ask me to dinner then give me no good-night kiss. You kiss me in the moonlight, then ignore me. If you don't want more than friendship, I—"

"Of course I do," he interrupted.

"Well, you've got a funny way of showing it." She must have seen something in his expression because she poked her index finger into his chest and said, "Don't you dare tell me it's complicated."

"You said you could handle the truth," he reminded her.

"I can. But it's really simple. Either you feel something for me or you don't. Clearly you don't. And I'm leaving before this gets even more weird."

"Don't go." Brendan took her hand to stop her. He stared into eyes so clear and blue and innocent they could wash away all the bad he carried inside him. He took a lock of her fiery hair between his fingers and breathed in the sweet, flowery scent of her skin. He'd used up every last ounce of willpower he had resisting the urge to have her. "Do you really not know that I think you're the most beautiful woman I've ever seen?"

Her smile was slow and sweet, but she wasn't quite sure of herself. "You do?"

"Seriously? Yes." He stared at her flawless face, cute little turned-up nose, full lips. "You're killing me here, Fee."

"So, what is it you want?" She studied him, searching for the answer on his face. "I don't mean the future. I'm not talking about tomorrow or the next day. What do you want now? Right this minute."

"You." The single word came out on a whisper as his heart pounded.

She moved closer so that their bodies were touching from chest to knee. Turning her face up, she asked, "Then what are you waiting for?"

Brendan knew he had good reasons for holding back, but right this second he had no idea what they were. He touched his mouth to hers and eagerly took what she offered. Her lips were soft and every bit as sexy here with the sun shining as they'd been in the moonlight.

He traced her mouth with his tongue and she opened to him without hesitation, offering everything. He explored slowly, thoroughly, and it wasn't nearly enough. He tugged her cotton shirt from the waistband of her jeans and slipped his hand underneath, settling his palm on her bare back. Her skin was even softer than he'd imagined and his imagination had gone wild. He moved his palm to her waist and slowly slid upward, brushing his thumb to the underside of her breast.

"Oh, Brendan—" Her breathing quickened and she pulled his shirt free from his jeans, then reached underneath, skimming her hands over his abdomen and up to his chest.

She seemed frustrated, in the cutest possible way, and tugged his snap-front shirt open. Pressing her body to his, she put her arms around his neck and stood on tiptoe to kiss him until he was sure his head was going to explode.

Brendan was breathing hard when he cupped her butt in his hands, then slid them to the backs of her thighs and lifted her. She wrapped her legs around his hips and he braced her against the tree, letting his forearm shield her back from the rough bark. If they didn't have their clothes on, he'd be inside her right now. He would—

Then the truth smacked him upside the head. Reality was a bitch. It was in the top ten hardest things he'd ever done, but Brendan pulled his mouth from hers.

"Fiona—"

"What?" Her voice was a breathless whisper, but there was wariness, too.

"You know I want you more than anything, right?"

"A second ago I thought so, but now I'm not so sure." She pressed her kiss-swollen lips together and there was a bruised expression in her eyes, as if she was expecting to be disappointed.

"It's the honest to God truth that I want you so much it hurts."

"But?"

"I don't have a condom."

She blinked at him as the consequences of that sank in. "Oh…"

He could almost see the wheels turning in her head and had a feeling he knew what she was about to suggest. He put a finger to her lips to stop the words. "No. I would never risk you that way. Besides, we're right out in the open. Not that far from Sunshine Farm. There's no telling who could ride by. I won't put you in a position like that."

"You're a good man." After blowing out a long breath she kissed his cheek. Then she let her legs slide down over his thighs until her boots touched the ground. "So, we're not that far from your cabin. Do you have protection there?"

He'd resigned himself to the fact that this wasn't going to happen. What with blood flow to his brain detoured, it took a second for her question to sink in. When it did, he grinned. "Why, yes, I do."

"Like I said, good man. I'll race you." She gave him a sassy look, then slipped out of his arms and sprinted toward the horses.

"Hot damn." Brendan was right behind her.

On horseback Fiona followed Brendan until he stopped in front of one of the seven log cabins built on Sunshine Farm property. It was small, and judging by the speed at which he dismounted, Brendan was in a hurry to get inside.

"I'll take care of the horses later." He took her reins

and along with his own tied them to one of the vertical log poles supporting the porch roof.

Fiona slid out of the saddle and met his gaze. His green eyes were more intense than she'd ever seen them and all the heat there was focused on her. But there was a question, too. And she didn't have to ask what it was.

She moved to him and slid her hand into his. "I haven't changed my mind."

A slow, sexy smile curved up the corners of his mouth. "It's been a long time."

That made her heart happy. Still, she couldn't resist saying, "I'm sure everything will come back to you."

With her hand tucked securely in his much larger one, they walked inside and shut the door behind them. It was barely closed before he pulled her into his arms and kissed her as if today was their last day on earth. In a heartbeat her breathing went from slightly elevated to "can't get enough air." The ride back had not cooled off her hormones. If anything, waiting made her want him even more desperately. She pulled at the snap front of his shirt, baring his chest to her touch. Again.

"Bedroom—that way," he said hoarsely, tugging her with him.

In the small room, simple cotton curtains covered the windows but sunlight sneaked in around the edges. There was a bed, a pine dresser and matching nightstands. In a frenzy they toed off boots and yanked off clothes, not necessarily their own. Brendan pulled the bedspread and blanket to the foot of the bed, then lifted her easily into his arms and set her in the middle of it.

He slid in beside her, then drew her to him and claimed her mouth. Her bare breasts were snuggled to his wide chest and she settled her palms on his back, exploring the impressive muscles. He swept his hand down her side and over her hip, the touch setting her on fire everywhere. But that was nothing compared to what she felt when his fingers trailed over her abdomen to the most intimate place between her thighs. If she was on fire before, now her body was an out-of-control blaze.

"Oh, God, Brendan. I want you…" She dug her fingers into the thick muscles of his biceps.

"Understood."

He rolled away, just far enough to reach into the nightstand and fumble around until he found what he was looking for. He retrieved the square packet and tore it open, then put on the condom.

He took her in his arms again and gently pressed her body into the mattress with his own. After nudging her legs apart with his knee, he slowly entered her and took his weight on his forearms. He was breathing really hard.

"Fiona—" he whispered.

"Yes." She arched her hips upward, showing him what she wanted without words.

He got the message. Slowly at first, then increasing the tempo, he thrust into her. With every movement she felt the tension tighten inside her until all too soon it exploded in a blaze of exquisite pleasure. He held her until the aftershocks subsided, then started to move again. One thrust, then another and another until he buried his face in her neck as he found his own release. She held him tight while his breathing slowed.

Finally he lifted his head and looked at her, then brushed the hair back from her face. His smile was soft, tender—peaceful. "I don't ever want to move."

"Me, either." She traced a finger over his chest, really liking the masculine dusting of hair. "I hear a 'but.'"

"The horses are still outside in front of the cabin."

As the reality sank in, her eyes widened. She'd been in too much of a hurry before to worry about being seen, but that changed in a heartbeat. If no one knew about them, they wouldn't talk. Or judge. "Holy Mother of God—"

"Yeah." He rolled away from her and got up, heading for the small bathroom.

She jumped out of bed and started getting dressed. "What if someone sees them? They'll know we—you—I—"

"Had sex." He came out of the bathroom still naked and all male perfection.

The extra pounds she carried had never bothered Fiona more than they did right this minute. But that was sort of like shutting the barn door after the horse got out. "I would prefer it if only you and I knew what happened."

"My lips are sealed," he agreed.

"I'm pretty sure we can count on the horses not to rat us out, but if anyone comes by and starts asking questions—"

"I suggest we get a move on before that happens." He came close and gave her a quick kiss before putting his clothes on.

After Fiona tucked in her shirt and finger-combed her hair, she said, "This will have to do."

"You look beautiful. Like you just came from a man's bed after—"

"Oh, God."

"Or back from a ride."

"Right," she said enthusiastically. "That would explain the messy hair."

Brendan opened the door and Fiona poked her head out, making sure the coast was clear for a clean getaway. There was no one in sight and she untied the reins of her horse. Brendan did the same and they started walking the animals to the barn for food, water and a rubdown.

She was rocking a nice little glow now that no one was the wiser about them having sex. The sky looked bluer. The air was fresher. Life was better. But when they were almost to the big yellow barn, Luke Stockton came around the corner and there was a man with him. She recognized Forrest Traub. The hunky former soldier walked with a limp, the result of being wounded in Iraq. He lived in Thunder Canyon, so the question was—why was he here?

"Hey, you two, how was the ride?" Luke asked.

Fiona felt heat creep into her cheeks. Did he know what they'd just done? Surely not. How could he? There was no choice but to brazen it out. "It was good. Beautiful day. Sun shining. Air crisp and clean. I brought over my mother's waffle iron. It wouldn't heat. Brendan fixed it." She was babbling and couldn't seem to stop. "Hey, Forrest. How are you? How's Angie?"

"My wife is great." He looked at the man beside her. "Who's your friend?"

More than a friend, she thought. But exactly what he was, she really had no idea. "Sorry. Where are my manners? This is Brendan Tanner."

"He's the guy I told you about," Luke said.

"Ex-marine." Forrest nodded. "I was army."

They talked a bit, and after Brendan told him about his father, the other man looked at him sympathetically.

"Sorry." He shifted his weight from one leg to the other and winced from the movement. "It's tough enough to readjust, but that's a really crappy thing to come home to."

"Yeah."

Fiona waited, but he didn't elaborate. Didn't explain that his adjustment didn't really start until after his dad died, making it feel pretty current to him. What was he thinking right now? He'd told her he hadn't figured out his future yet. Was he wishing he was still in the military? The subtext of what he'd said was that he hadn't wanted to resign but was forced to by his father's illness.

"Brendan is actually why I asked Forrest to come and check out Sunshine Farm," Luke said.

"Oh?" Fiona wasn't following.

"From experience I understand the challenges of reintegrating to civilian life," Forrest said. "Especially when there are physical changes. I had a hard time. Bitter and angry. If not for Angie I don't know where I'd be right now." He shook his head. "And I came home with just a bum leg. Some men and women have it really hard. Missing limbs. Traumatic brain injury. Then there are the emotional wounds of PTSD. Mental challenges can often be harder to measure progress."

"I'm not sure where Sunshine Farm comes in," she admitted.

"Luke contacted me because he knows I work with returning veterans and groups that help them assimilate to life stateside. He thinks a stay here might help a veteran dealing with all kinds of war-related problems."

"You'd have to ask Brendan to confirm," Luke said, "but I think R & R here has made him a little more social."

"Are you serious? Rest and relaxation?" Brendan laughed. "He's got the whole town bringing me stuff to fix. On top of that I get a call every day about fixing ranch equipment. Now he's nagging me to open a business. It's been nothing but work."

"And yet you continue to do it." Luke nodded with satisfaction. "So that got me to thinking. There are seven cabins. I helped my dad build them—one for each of his kids." Satisfaction faded and there was sadness in his eyes. "He and my mom wanted all of us to live here. If that didn't work out, they said they could always open a dude ranch."

"It didn't quite go that way," Fiona said gently.

Everyone in Rust Creek Falls knew the story. His folks died too young in a car accident, and the family got split up. Some of their kids were pretty little and ended up getting adopted by other families. The older boys—including Luke—left town on their own, and the rest were raised by their grandparents. In the last couple of years the Stocktons were finding their way back to each other.

"So what's your plan for the cabins?" she asked.

"I want to dedicate a couple of them for veterans who might need a quiet place where they can get a fresh start." He stopped for a moment. "I've given this a lot of thought and I'd like to start a charitable foundation, add more cabins. Make the existing ones more homey. But that would take some money."

"Hey, this is Rust Creek Falls. People are generous and more than happy to contribute to a good cause," Fiona pointed out. "In fact, you guys are having a Halloween party here, right?"

"Yeah," he said. "We want to make it an annual family tradition."

"Turn it into a fund-raiser," she suggested. "I'll get the word out on that. We can do a bake sale and pass the hat. All you and Eva have to do is plan the party, which I'm quite sure she has under control. Let me do the rest."

"Are you sure?" Luke said.

"Yes."

"Okay, then. I knew I could count on you. Everyone does."

Not everyone, she thought, looking up at Brendan. He

might be more social than when he got here, but he was still holding part of himself back. After what they'd just done in his cabin, she was more emotionally invested than she wanted to be. Obviously he was attracted to her, but he'd come right out and said he wouldn't make promises. There was every reason to believe she was just spinning her wheels.

Chapter Nine

For Brendan, time was now defined as before sleeping with Fiona and after. Before yesterday he'd been able to tell himself he could resist her. Today that didn't hold water. He couldn't stop thinking about her. Had sex ever been that perfect? Or was it just perfect with her?

And, damn it, how long had he been staring into space picturing her naked? If the guys in his unit could see him now, he'd be mocked mercilessly. *Back to work*, he told himself.

He looked at the broken toaster he'd taken apart and the line of small appliances on the workbench—some fixed, some waiting for his attention. He had decided to take a day off from fixing ranch equipment and try to clear off a backlog of things that folks needed in their homes. The sheer number was impressive and each one represented people who'd reached out to him.

"This town is sucking me in," he grumbled.

And not just the town. Fiona.

She was sassy and strong. Independent. And that was sexy as hell. The only part of making love to her that didn't meet a perfect standard was having to get up to care for the horses. But doing that first wasn't an option.

He'd nearly taken her by the stream. Waiting to have her was the hardest thing he'd ever done. The idea of not leaving his bed and making love to her for a week was awfully appealing, but he had a feeling even that wouldn't be long enough. And he was off again, thinking about her in his arms.

"I'm going to start calling you Sergeant Slacker." Luke walked into the workshop and set a large cardboard box on the bench in front of Brendan.

"That's Sergeant Major Slacker to you, and I'm going as fast as I can," he lied. Apparently he didn't need the guys in his old unit to mock him. Luke filled that role just fine.

"I would hope so." The other man grinned. "Because I have an idea."

"Does this inspiration have anything to do with me?"

"What was your first clue?"

"I'm pretty sure you didn't come out here to insult my work ethic." He nodded at the box in front of him. "And you brought a whole bunch of junk."

"Of all people you should see the potential here." Luke picked up a remote control car that had seen better days. "If you can fix this, it's worth something to someone. That would be found money. Maybe that's why it's called a *foundation*."

"Funny guy." Brendan glanced down at the box's contents and saw a stuffed toy with a pull on the back that presumably had made it talk at one time. There was a mirror with lights around it. If they lit up the thing wouldn't be here. And he saw a mobile with zoo animals hanging from a windup thing, for a baby's crib. "So you plan to sell these."

"If you can fix them. And I have every faith you can. Obviously you'd be donating your time," he pointed out.

"And just when am I supposed to find time to donate? What with making house calls to ranches to repair the big-ticket machinery?"

"You can teach someone how to do what you do."

The way his father had taught him, Brendan thought. "Are you planning to set up a booth in the corral to sell this stuff?"

Luke didn't look at all discouraged. "I'm going to search for retail space in town. Maybe I can talk the owner into reduced rent, or better yet, none at all, to maximize profits. Eva and I have big plans for Sunshine Farm. People coming here for a fresh start might be willing to volunteer some time, or if things go well, we can afford to pay a wage for their work."

"An awful lot of things have to fall into place," he pointed out.

"You are so glass-half-empty." Luke *tsk*ed. "Have some faith."

"I do. Faith that I may not be sticking around."

"And leave all this?" His friend glanced around the workshop that was starting to look like a trash heap with bicycles in various stages of disrepair. An electric frying pan and Crock-Pot were gathering dust. There was a leaf blower and even a chainsaw someone had persuaded him to try to work a miracle on.

"Hard to believe, I know," Brendan said wryly.

"Seriously, you should open a repair shop in town, right next to the Sunshine Farm Foundation Store. There's a real need and you'd be doing something worthwhile. It's a win-win."

"This was never a career goal," he pointed out. "Just something to keep me busy."

"Mission accomplished." Luke folded his arms over

his chest. "A man can't spend all his time on keeping in shape, you know."

That was a reference to his daily workouts. Training had been hit-and-miss when he was caring for his dad. Since coming to Rust Creek Falls, his daily routine included intense exercise in order to be physically ready to reenlist.

"I don't want folks to start depending on me."

"Hate to break it to you, my friend. They already do."

But could he depend on them? Before joining the Marines, the only person Brendan trusted was his dad.

In the military, shared experiences, hardship and danger had forged unbreakable bonds, ones that made his fellow soldiers more like brothers. But civilian life had not given him any reason to trust people.

Luke sighed. "At least think about making it permanent?"

Maybe that would keep him from thinking about Fiona. "Will do."

"So, when I walked in here just now you were deep in thought. Did that have anything to do with a certain pretty redhead who volunteered to handle the Halloween party fund-raiser for the foundation?"

It was like the man could read his mind and Brendan wasn't comfortable with that. On the day of his horseback ride with Fiona, Brendan remembered that his friend had said he was partially responsible for the idea to dedicate a certain number of cabins for soldiers. Brendan didn't want to be anyone's poster boy.

"I have a lot of things on my mind," he said.

"Are all of them named Fiona?"

The man wasn't going to let this go so it might be good to just throw him a bone. "She's a very special woman."

"You'll get no argument from me. Is it my imagination

that things have gotten serious between you two pretty quickly?"

As much as Brendan wanted to push back against that, he couldn't. That was the truth. And sleeping with her complicated everything. He hadn't changed his mind about her being the kind of woman who deserved more than a one-night stand.

"Are you asking me what my intentions are?"

"No. Yes." Luke held up a hand to stop the angry reply he was expecting. "I know I have no right. She's a grown woman, but—"

"You feel like a brother to her," Brendan finished.

"Yeah. How did you know that?"

"She told me it's hard to meet men in Rust Creek Falls because she grew up with most of them and they're all like brothers." He also knew that Fiona wasn't a fan of anyone fixing her up.

"Since I left town for years I didn't exactly grow up with her." Luke's easygoing expression disappeared for a moment, but then he seemed to shake off whatever had put it there. "Call me a cockeyed optimist—"

"You're a cockeyed optimist."

The other man laughed. "But I want everyone to be as happy as Eva and I are."

"You guys are the lucky ones."

His father hadn't been, and Leon warned Brendan not to risk his heart. So far he'd been pretty successful. Love had never been an issue because he always kept women at a distance. Somehow Fiona had breached his perimeter without firing a shot—just by being her. And suddenly the rules of engagement made no sense to him anymore.

"I am lucky," Luke agreed.

"For some of us that's just not in the cards."

"Then some of you have to make an effort to turn over

different cards." He held up a hand again. "I'm not asking why, just saying you don't have to be alone."

He'd always felt alone but that was before Fiona. And he'd never missed any woman the way he did her when they were apart. But putting up barriers was second nature now. Bringing them down wasn't easy to do and he wasn't even sure he wanted to try.

"Look, not that I don't enjoy being badgered," Brendan said, "but don't you have something else to do? Somewhere else to be? Another guy to play matchmaker for? And it has to be said. I'm not sure the Cupid thing is a good look for you."

"I'm really hurt," Luke teased. "But you're not wrong. I do have to get going. As a matter of fact, I'm on my way into town and, if you want, I can deliver some of the things you've repaired. Save you a trip."

"That's okay. I'll take care of it." His response was automatic, a default position, not depending on anyone. If he did it himself, he knew the job was done. No one could let him down. "Thanks for the offer, though."

"We're going to have to learn to work together when you eventually crack under pressure and agree to open the repair shop. When that happens, I promise not to say I told you so."

Before Brendan could tell him he was full of it, Luke walked away. Based on the man's perceptive remarks about Fiona and his own tendency to distrust others, it was hard not to believe that Luke was reading his mind.

Except if that was the case, he would also know why he felt the way he did. In the Marines, it started with boot camp. Recruits had to work together. If someone screwed up they were all punished. Others had his back; he had theirs. The training prepared them all for what was coming and the bond became stronger, literally forged in fire, during the heat of battle.

He'd never felt like he belonged anywhere the way he did in the Marine Corps. Brendan had made it through his father's illness and passing because of his resolve to reenlist when he got himself in good enough physical shape.

Then Fiona chased a kid into this workshop and his whole world tilted. The more time he spent with her, the more he felt caught in a firefight without his combat armor. It was easy for Luke to hype being married when things worked out so well for him. But Brendan had seen what happened when it all went to hell and he didn't want to set foot in that minefield.

After learning of Luke Stockton's plans for Sunshine Farm and the foundation he planned to start, Fiona got busy. The Halloween party was coming up fast and she had to get word out quickly. So, late the following afternoon, she headed to *The Rust Creek Falls Gazette* office in town. The sooner there was a notice in the paper, the better.

She needed to see the features editor, Nell Cook, who was in charge of a page called "What's Cookin'." She reported upcoming town events and a calendar of activities. If there was a bake sale, car wash for charity or a health clinic, Nell handled it. But she couldn't do that if she didn't know about it.

The office was located on North Main Street, and Fiona drove into the parking lot it shared with Bee's Beauty Parlor, Wings To Go and Daisy's Donuts. All of these businesses fronted the parallel street, North Broomtail Road. She parked and slid out of the truck, then headed around the building to the front door.

Nell was her friend. They'd gone to high school together, but the other woman was a couple of years younger. She wasn't married yet, either, but at least the big 3-0 wasn't staring *her* in the face.

Lydia Grant, receptionist and editor, sat at the front desk. She smiled. "Hi, Fiona. Go on back. Nell won't mind."

"Thanks."

She went down the short hall and found her friend's office. The door was open and Nell's back was to it. She was staring intently at the computer monitor.

Fiona knocked once. "What's cookin'?"

The other woman swiveled her chair around and grinned, then stood and walked past the cluttered desk for a hug. "Like I've never heard that before."

"Yeah. I couldn't resist. How are you?" She glanced at the desktop chaos that somehow worked for her friend. "Looks like you're keeping busy."

"That's an understatement," said the pretty brown-eyed brunette. "And you're here to give me more work, aren't you?"

"How did you know?"

"Because I know *you*. Have a seat." She indicated the unpadded chair and rested a hip on the corner of her desk, probably the only spot without something on it. "What's up?"

"Luke Stockton is turning his Halloween party into a fund-raiser."

"For what?"

"You're going to who, what, when, where and why me, so just listen without interrupting and I'll give it to you all at once." She took a deep breath and filled in her friend on all of Luke's plans. "Actually it was my idea to make a fund-raiser out of the Halloween party he and Eva are having at Sunshine Farm."

"You mean Lonelyhearts Ranch?" she said with a laugh.

"No. Officially it's called Sunshine Farm. And you can't miss the big yellow barn it gets its name from."

"That barn is visible from the moon," Nell agreed. "But the name Lonelyhearts Ranch is catching fire. As are the people who stay there, it would seem." She sighed at Fiona's look. "Don't pretend you don't know what I'm talking about. I don't write 'Rust Creek Ramblings' but I never miss a column that publicizes what goes on in this town."

"Me, either." The column contained gossip, rumors and romantic liaisons and was not to be missed. No one in town wanted to be left out of the loop. But Fiona wanted to be left out of any talk that could land her in that column. "I've noticed that fresh starters at the ranch have been featured a little."

"A little?" Nell pushed her black-framed glasses to the top of her head. "You think?"

Fiona knew her friend was driving at something but she couldn't see what. "It's all about a safe place to get your life together."

"Hmm." The other woman nodded knowingly. "Finding a relationship could also be defined as 'getting your life together.'"

"It's not about falling in love." If it were, Fiona would know.

"Maybe not about that, but it's still going on."

"What are you talking about?" That was a stall because Fiona knew exactly what she meant.

"Luke and Eva." Nell held up a hand and started counting off fingers.

"Technically they fell in love before moving to the ranch."

The other woman continued as if she hadn't said anything. "Amy Wainwright, who came for their wedding fell back in love with Derek Dalton. Or maybe they never stopped loving each other since that secret, impulsive teenage marriage."

"So the ranch didn't have anything to do with them committing to each other," Fiona argued.

"But it came together for them while Amy was staying there." She held up a third finger. "Then there's Mikayla Brown, who came to stay. Even pregnant, or maybe because she was, she ended up with millionaire Jensen Jones."

"Okay. I'll give you that. But it's coincidence that she happened to be staying there."

Wagging her ring finger, Nell said, "Josselyn Weaver came to stay and ended up with delicious widower Dr. Drew Strickland. She just came for a new beginning and found it with the doctor and his son."

"So she wasn't a lonely heart running from something." But Fiona had a feeling she was spitting into the wind.

"I'm beginning to think there's something in the water there, or a romantic vibe. So far everyone who came to visit has fallen in love."

"What's your point, Nell?"

"Brendan Tanner." There was a gleam in her eyes.

"It's certainly no secret that he's staying there." Fiona knew she was being guarded, but this conversation was headed to a place she didn't want to go.

"My point is—what's up with you and Brendan?"

"We've met."

"That's usually a prerequisite for something being up," Nell said wryly. "There's a rumor that you two are more than acquaintances."

Eva and Luke would know they'd hung out. Her parents and brothers, too. That meant her sisters, Fallon and Brenna, could know and say something to their husbands. Any one of them could have dropped a casual remark to anyone. In this town gossip spread fast, like fire in dry brush with hurricane force winds to push it along.

"Where did you hear that we're more than friends?"

"Around," the other woman said vaguely. "Is it true?"

"Is what true?"

"Oh, come on, Fiona. You know what I'm asking." She folded her arms over her chest. "Are you and Brendan Tanner an item?"

She did her best not to squirm in the uncomfortable chair under her friend's scrutiny. They knew each other so well it was possible Nell could see on Fiona's face that she'd done the wild thing with Brendan. "There is nothing but friendship between Brendan and me."

"You're lying. Something is up with you. What is it?"

"I feel like a witness on the stand. Since when is it your job to be the town's heart monitor?"

"Since you're my friend. And it's not the town's heart I'm concerned about. It's yours. I care about you." She shrugged. "Plus, I hear things."

"*Things* are thrown around in conversation every time someone in Rust Creek Falls goes into a store or business. How much of it is actually true?" Fiona argued.

"If you're talking about the Lonelyhearts Ranch, so far it's one hundred percent accurate."

The woman had a point. On top of everything else Fiona was wrestling with, she was going to have the distinction of being the first one to spoil that perfect romantic record. The quieter she kept whatever was happening with Brendan, the less likely she was to go down in Rust Creek Falls lore as a loser at love.

"Every streak comes to an end." Fiona did her best to keep her tone neutral.

"I haven't met him yet," Nell admitted. "Is he as good-looking as I've heard?"

Even better, she wanted to say. *And you should see him without his clothes on.* Sharing that, however, was not the way to avoid more personal questions. "He's very pretty, in a manly way."

"Where on the scale?"

Fiona knew she meant one to ten with ten being Hollywood-hunk gorgeous. "He's definitely above a five."

Nell removed her glasses from the top of her head and tossed them on a pile of papers littering the desk. "If I didn't know you better, I would say that you're trying to discourage me from checking him out. Is that because you've staked a claim?"

"No."

And even if she had, it would take two to be exclusive. Brendan obviously liked hanging out with her. She would have to be an idiot not to get that. But he never made a promise to her, so there'd been no vow to break. That would almost make it easier because then she could be angry. Anger was a very big shield to hide behind.

Fiona stood. "If you want to check him out, go for it. Be my guest. I have no objection."

"No, thanks." Nell grinned. "You of all people know that I don't have time for men."

What her friend meant was that she'd sworn off them, with good reason. "I better go. It's getting late. Do you want to go to Ace in the Hole for a burger?"

"If only." She sighed. "I have a lot of work here. Top on the list is writing up something about the Halloween party fund-raiser at Luke Stockton's place."

"I've never been more grateful that you're a worka-

holic. It's a really good thing he's going to do." Fiona
stood. "Thanks, Nell."

After a goodbye hug, Fiona left the building and went
to the parking lot. She glanced at the vehicles there and
noticed a familiar truck with Texas plates in a Marine
Corps frame. It was in a space right by Daisy's Donuts.

And suddenly she had a very strong craving for sugar.

Chapter Ten

Brendan's last delivery of the day was a repaired toaster oven. After reluctantly accepting payment, he walked away with a broken vacuum cleaner. He put it in the rear passenger section of his truck with the other things folks had given him to fix. It seemed customer satisfaction was so high he had as many broken items as before, and that didn't include the list of ranch jobs he'd promised to do. Job security if he wanted it.

The last stop had been on North Broomtail Road, and Daisy's Donuts was ahead on the right. He knew he could get a cup of coffee there and that sounded pretty good right about now. So he pulled into the lot behind the store and parked. As he walked inside, the sweet baked goods smell made his stomach rumble. He couldn't remember whether or not he'd eaten lunch.

This was where Eva Stockton worked, doing the baking, but he didn't think she'd be here now. Since it was coming up on dinnertime, most likely she would be home, cooking for her husband.

A feeling of loneliness seasoned with a dash of envy rolled through him. It was a little surprising that he so quickly recognized the emotions since they were rare for

him. He'd always been a little smug about having everything he needed. Then he came to Sunshine Farm and realized he had nothing. That was another reason why he
was leaning toward reenlistment.

He glanced around at the empty tables of the shop and
at the glass display case. There weren't many customers
this late in the day. Before he could approach the counter,
the bell tinkled over the door he'd just walked through.

Automatically he turned to see who came in and recognized Fiona. He was really happy to see her, no two
ways about it. Loneliness retreated and her sunny smile
chased away the darkness. A man could get used to that.
In fact, every time he saw her it was like the first time,
when he felt as if he'd been smacked upside the head with
a two-by-four. In a good way.

He was grinning like a fool and didn't care. Maybe it
was low blood sugar. "Hi."

"I thought that was your truck in the parking lot." She
moved close and looked up at him. "In Montana a Texas
license plate sticks out like a fly in milk."

"So this isn't a coincidence."

"Only in the sense that I was at the newspaper the same
time you stopped here," she said.

So it had been deliberate on her part to come inside
and see him. The fact that she'd made the effort had him
feeling pretty doggone good.

"What were you doing at the *Gazette*?"

"I'm following up on my promise to Luke—to orga-
nize his first annual Halloween party fund-raiser." She
glanced through the big window to the newspaper building across the parking lot. "Every edition of the paper has
a list of what's going on here in town. My friend works
there. She'll give Luke's foundation benefit good play."

"You didn't waste any time."

"There isn't any to waste," she said. "It's right around the corner."

And the idea for it had gone down yesterday. Right after he'd made love to her. Brendan felt a hitch in his breathing and fought the urge to pull her into his arms now. But this was Daisy's Donuts, not an isolated, sun-drenched meadow overlooking a river. That one time was a slip-up. It wasn't fair to put her in that position again. Not when his future was unsettled. He wouldn't be another jerk who led her on, then walked away and hurt her.

"Hey, Tanner. You listening?"

"Hmm?" He reeled in his thoughts and saw Fiona angle her head toward the blonde teenage girl watching the shop and patiently waiting for him to order something. "Can I buy you a cup of coffee?"

"Sure."

Together they walked over to the low counter beside the glass display case. "Two coffees, please."

"Anything to go with that? Cookie? Donut? Muffin?" The blonde looked about twelve but had to be older than that to work here.

"Do you want something?" he asked Fiona.

"So very much." She sighed. "But no. Just coffee."

"Nothing else," he told the teen.

"Okay." She filled two cups and made change when Brendan paid. "Coffee stuff is over there."

Fiona took her coffee, moved to a table not in front of a window and sat down.

Brendan joined her and took the seat across from her. "No 'stuff' for you?"

"I learned to drink it black. Easier when you have to get up before God in the morning."

"Me, too."

"No sissy coffee for you?" she teased.

"That's one way to put it." Places he'd been while in the Marines didn't have frills, so black it was.

"What brings you into town?" She blew on the coffee, dispersing the steam. The movement made her lips pucker and all he could think about was how much he wanted to kiss her.

"Deliveries." His voice was hoarse so he cleared his throat. "I returned small appliances that I fixed."

"So you don't make people pick them up. Great customer service."

He shrugged. "They could if there was a rush. Otherwise I'm happy to drop them off."

"And then you needed coffee. Is it safe to assume you're so busy that the abundance of work wore you out?"

That was partly true. The other part had to do with a lousy night's sleep because he couldn't stop thinking of her in his bed and wishing she'd never left. But he only said, "Business has been good."

"So, has Luke said 'I told you so' yet?"

"No." The man only said people were starting to depend on Brendan, which might be worse. And clearly his friend hadn't given up on the fix-it shop. He told Fiona about Luke's idea of going mobile for dishwashers and refrigerators, and how he was thinking about turning trashed items into profit to benefit the foundation. "I'll admit he may be onto something. A shop like that could turn into a profitable business in Rust Creek Falls."

"Not just anyone could make it successful," she pointed out.

Only *he* could do that, was what she meant. The work made him feel good, which surprised him because he'd felt just the opposite when he was a kid. He'd been ashamed that he never had anything new. His dad cobbled things together, including a life after his mother left.

There'd been another woman for a couple of years and Brendan had gotten a taste of what a family might feel like. But it didn't last. In his experience, the only place he was guaranteed to fit in was the Marine Corps. In the military he knew he would have a place to belong, be a part of a family.

But sitting across from Fiona was temptation on steroids. She was the kind of woman his father had warned him to guard his heart against. A pretty, practical, down-to-earth woman who could make him want to give her everything, then yank the rug out from underneath him. The kind he would miss for the rest of his life.

He sipped his coffee and thought about her words. Only he could make a fix-it business successful. The question was whether or not he wanted to try. He didn't know the answer and wanted to shelve the subject. So that's what he did.

"How have you been?" he asked.

"You mean since yesterday?" The thing about a redhead's skin was not being able to hide a blush.

He really liked the way the high color made her eyes bluer and put a sparkle in them. "Yeah, since then."

Her expression turned a little shy and it was a good guess that she was thinking about what they'd done in his cabin. But she met his look directly. "I've been really good. How about you?"

"Fine." A lousy night's sleep didn't count. "Like I said. Busy."

"Me, too. In between ranch chores I sold another article."

"Which one?"

"The one I was telling you about. How to survive a Montana winter."

"And how does one do that?" he asked.

"Find a way to stay warm." Her eyes went all smoky and soft and it looked like she meant sharing body heat. In a naked sort of way.

Or maybe she hadn't meant that at all. Could be his imagination was overheated. Before he had a chance to decide which, he realized the donut shop teenager was clearing her throat, trying to get their attention. That's when he saw that the glass case had been emptied and the lights behind the counter were off.

"I'm sorry, but it's time to close up now," the teen said.

Fiona stood and carried her empty cup to the trash can. "I didn't realize. We didn't mean to keep you late."

"I normally wouldn't care, but it's a school night and I have to get home and do schoolwork." She looked apologetic.

"We are out of here." Brendan put his cup in the trash by the door. "Thanks for letting us stay awhile."

"No problem. Come back again."

"Will do."

He held the door for Fiona as they walked outside. The air was crisp and cold, a prelude to the Montana winter she had been talking about surviving. She was going to get in her truck and he'd get in his and that would be that. Saved from naked body heat.

But a feeling took hold and wouldn't let go. He just didn't want to spend another evening alone in his cabin. Not if there was a chance of spending it with her. Even fully clothed.

He put a hand on her arm to keep her from walking away. "How would you feel about going to Ace in the Hole for a beer and a bite to eat?"

"I wouldn't like to go alone."

"Smart-ass." He must be way out of practice with this

stuff. Asking a woman to eat with him shouldn't be this hard. "I was wondering if you would go with me."

"In that case, I would enjoy it very much."

That's when he turned to rationalization to justify his lapse in willpower. Lately he was very good at rationalizing. He told himself he and Fiona were just two friends having a burger together. No big deal. It was a public place. Nothing would happen.

Fiona rode to Ace in the Hole with Brendan and was pretty happy that he'd invited her along. And just a little proud of herself for taking the initiative to say hello to him in Daisy's Donuts. The evening couldn't have turned out better if she'd planned it.

After doing a mental high five, she smiled sweetly at him from the truck's passenger seat. "I didn't expect to see you so soon. It was a nice coincidence, us being in town at the same time."

"My good luck." In the light from the dashboard, his grin was clearly visible.

The words made her glow almost as brightly as she had in his bed. Then, after talking to Luke Stockton and Forrest Traub yesterday, she'd gone home without anyone the wiser. But there'd been no promise of a phone call or date. Then they both ended up in the same parking lot at the same time, so who was she to spit in fate's eye?

The drive took only a few minutes and she was almost disappointed when the neon beer sign in the window of the local cowboy bar came into view. Also on display was the big ace of hearts playing card that gave the place its name.

Brendan pulled the truck into the lot and parked. "There are quite a few people here on a weeknight."

"It's a popular place." She was reluctant to give up

the intimacy of being alone with him, but hunger won out. "Let's go."

After exiting the truck, they walked side by side to the entrance, and he opened the squeaky screen door for her. The interior was dimly lighted but she knew this place like the back of her hand. Tables and chairs were arranged on the wood plank floor to form a dance area and there were booths around the perimeter of the large room. An oak bar, scratched and scarred from years of use, took up one wall. Halloween decorations were evidence that trick-or-treat time was fast approaching. There was a plastic pumpkin sitting at one end of the bar and fake webs with plastic spiders sticking to the walls.

Brendan pointed. "Let's grab a booth."

"Okay." It was on the other side of the big room, a little more private than the tables near the dance floor.

He put his hand to the small of her back, and the pressure of his touch warmed her everywhere. They walked past a table where four women sat with drinks in front of them. A beautiful, slim blonde stared shamelessly at Brendan and there was no mistaking the flirtatious expression on her face.

Fiona glanced up at him to see if he'd noticed and his tense expression made her curious. "I bet that happens to you all the time."

"What?" He frowned at her.

"You walk into a room and have women eating out of your hand."

"First of all, it's less messy when people use plates. And second, someone that obvious isn't a person I want to get to know."

"So you did notice the ogling."

"Seriously?" His voice was teasing. "Survival training

stresses close observation of your surroundings. I was a marine. It's a hard habit to break."

"Who knew your survival skills would come in handy for civilian life?"

"Identify and evade," he said. "Sometimes it's the best way to avoid awkward, messy situations."

Interesting, Fiona thought. She guessed that he didn't like rejecting someone. To be fair, most people didn't, but if she had to speculate, the process made him acutely uncomfortable. Since Fiona was with him, her presence should keep in check any unwanted attention.

They left Ms. Ogler behind and slid into the booth across from each other. It wasn't more than a minute or two before Rosey Traven appeared. The sixtyish owner of the Ace wore a peasant blouse that revealed a hint of her ample bosom and was cinched at her waist with a wide leather belt. Her dark blue jeans were tight and she wore red cowboy boots.

"Fiona O'Reilly. I haven't seen you in forever. Almost forgot what you look like."

"Hey, Rosey." Ace in the Hole didn't have the best memories for her, what with this being where Ronan met the jerk he introduced her to, the one who broke her heart. Coming with Brendan might cancel it out. She opened her mouth to introduce him but Rosey was already talking.

"Brendan Tanner." The older woman smiled at him. Clearly they'd met. "Good to see you again."

"Same here. Where's your husband?"

"You met Sam?" Fiona asked.

Rosey laughed. "My husband knew this man was military as soon as he walked in."

"Sam was a navy SEAL," Brendan explained.

"I actually knew that," Fiona said wryly.

"Sam took a fellow veteran under his wing and they

had a lot to talk about. He's in the back, organizing inventory. I'll send him out to say hello when he's free."

"I'd like that." Brendan seemed at ease with her.

"So, what can I get you two? Need a menu?"

"Not me," Fiona said. "Burger, fries and a house cabernet."

"I'll have the same," Brendan said. "Except make it a draft beer."

"Coming right up." She glanced in the direction of the blonde who'd checked them out on the way in. "Didn't Paisley put the moves on you the last time you were here?"

"Yeah." His expression turned grim.

"Thought so." Rosey looked at him, then Fiona, as if she were sizing them up relationship-wise. But she didn't comment. "I'll send Jackie over with your drinks."

"Thanks, Rosey." When the woman walked away, Fiona met his gaze. "So you've been here before."

"Yeah. Nights get long and this is more my style than Maverick Manor."

She knew what he meant about this place being comfortable, like a broken-in saddle.

"Rosey and Sam are good people." And both of them had misjudged the jerk who romanced and rejected her. But he'd been a stranger and had fooled almost everyone. That tended to make a girl wary about someone who wasn't born and raised in Rust Creek Falls.

The young woman working the bar came over with a beer mug for him and a glass of wine for her. "Let me know if you want refills."

"Thanks." Brendan picked his glass up and took a sip. "Tastes good after a long, hard day."

Fiona sipped her own drink. "I'll second that."

They made small talk while waiting for food and, good

to her word, Rosey brought out two burger baskets in record time.

"Enjoy," she said, then moved away to chat with and check up on people at nearby tables.

Fiona ate a couple of fries to kill the hunger pains, then dug into the thick, messy hamburger. She'd eaten half of it before saying, "I'm too hungry to talk."

He pretended to be shocked. "Who are you and what have you done with Fiona O'Reilly? I thought you were all about conversation."

"I know. Priorities. Deal with it." She grinned before taking another bite.

Brendan was no slouch in putting away food, either. His disappeared even faster than hers. He pushed away the empty red plastic basket. "That was good."

After chewing the last bite of hamburger, Fiona finished up her fries and sighed. "Well, the way I wolfed that down was certainly not ladylike."

"Did you enjoy it?" he asked.

"So very much."

"Okay, then."

"Now that I'm full, I absolutely swear on Rosey's bar that I will lose the pesky extra pounds that are probably several more after what I just ate."

Brendan studied her as he toyed with the handle of his beer mug. He looked perplexed. "You don't need to lose weight."

Fiona figured he was just being nice since he'd seen her naked. "That's easy for you to say."

"The truth *is* easy," he insisted. "You are not overweight."

"I'm sure not slender like Brenna and Fallon."

"Your sisters aren't curvy and sexy like you. If I get a vote, I wouldn't change a single thing."

Fiona stared at him for several moments, not sure she'd heard him correctly. "You think I'm sexy?"

"Now you're just fishing for compliments," he teased.

"I'm really not. I sincerely want to know."

His eyes were suddenly hot and intense as he leaned forward. "I think you're damn sexy and so does every other man in here. All of them have been checking you out since we walked in. I'm not the only one getting ogled. Trust me on this, Fiona. You're the most beautiful woman in here. My humble opinion? You shouldn't mess with perfection. Stay just the way you are."

The words made Fiona go all warm and gooey inside. It could be insincere flattery. She'd been on the receiving end of that before. But then she realized that was her default skepticism kicking in. She'd bet that he wasn't a sweet talker. Heck, he wasn't much of a talker, period. Her heart melted like butter in a hot frying pan.

She'd been thrown off balance by his compliment and hadn't taken note of the jukebox playing. Some people were now using the dance floor.

"Are you in a hurry to leave?" Brendan asked.

"Are you?"

"Asked you first."

"Honestly, no. But if you're tired—"

"I'm not." He glanced over at the couples moving slowly to the ballad that was playing. "Would you like to dance?"

"Yes." More than her next breath she wanted to be in his arms again. For any reason at all.

He slid out of the booth and held out his hand to her. She took it and stood, then walked with him to the dance floor. He circled his arm around her waist and tucked her close to his body, then wrapped her hand in his and settled them on his chest. They swayed to the music, and

Fiona knew she would hold this perfect moment in her heart forever.

Too soon the song ended and they walked back to their booth. Before sitting Fiona said, "I'm going to the ladies' room. Be right back."

"I'll be here."

She smiled before heading past the end of the bar and into the hallway where the restrooms were located. The women's was blissfully quiet and she quickly took care of business and washed her hands. She'd forgotten her purse and couldn't reapply lip gloss, but Brendan had certainly seen her look worse. Roundup came to mind. And she smiled remembering what he'd said a little while ago.

You're the most beautiful woman in here... Stay just the way you are.

She was going to hold that in her heart forever, too, and pretty much every moment since she'd seen him at Daisy's Donuts She smiled happily and went back out into the hallway.

Rosey was standing by the end of the bar. "Look who moved in on your man."

She saw that Paisley woman talking to Brendan and a knot of fury coiled inside her. They were standing by the booth and he looked really uncomfortable. If the woman was an enemy combatant he would know exactly what to do. He was too much of a gentleman to tell her to get lost but Fiona wasn't too much of a lady. "He's not my man. But…"

Fiona didn't wait for Rosey's reply. She walked over and wrapped her arms around Brendan's waist, snuggling close, then smiled at the pretty blonde. "Hi. I'm Fiona. I don't think we've met."

"Paisley Ritter."

"Pretty name," she said sweetly. "I see you met my boyfriend, Brendan."

"Yes." The other woman didn't seem quite so chatty now.

"Would you like to join us for a drink?"

Paisley looked startled. "No. My friends are waiting."

Fiona rested her cheek against Brendan's chest. "If you change your mind, just come on over. Bring your friends, too."

"Okay. See you around." She didn't look at either of them before turning and scurrying away.

"Boyfriend, huh?" Brendan smiled down at her before kissing her lightly on the mouth. "You didn't even raise your voice."

"Didn't have to. Killed her with kindness. She never knew what hit her."

"They're leaving," he said, nodding toward Paisley and her friends, who were walking out the door.

"You're welcome."

"Seriously, thanks. You have no idea how grateful I am."

"I've got your back," she assured him. *Always*, she added silently.

"I owe you big-time."

"And I know just how you can pay me back. A *boyfriend* usually comes to dinner with family. And my mother wants to thank you for fixing her waffle iron. How about tomorrow night?"

He looked like he would rather take a sharp stick in the eye, but answered like the brave soldier he was. "I would love to."

Fiona wasn't sure why that's what she wanted as a thank-you except maybe so he'd be less of a stranger. It was becoming more important to her that he lose the label.

Chapter Eleven

At five minutes to six the next evening, Brendan turned onto the road that led to the Rusty Bucket Ranch. The last time he'd been here it was to pick up Fiona for dinner. It was quick and almost painless. Tonight he was staying. All he could say was, the next time he told someone "I owe you," he would find out what paying off the debt entailed. Her brothers hated him and the jury was out on her father. Her mother seemed nice. Maybe she could hold off the men if things went sideways.

What bothered him more than an evening with two hostile older brothers was that he couldn't say no to Fiona. He was pretty sure that he would have agreed to this dinner invitation whether he owed her or not. Just because she asked.

That's as far as he would go with that thought. Anything more made him feel too exposed when he was about to face the O'Reilly men on their territory.

At six o'clock on the dot he pulled the truck to a stop in front of Fiona's house, where lights were ablaze in all the downstairs windows. "Here goes nothing," he muttered.

All his senses were on high alert, not unlike the way he'd felt on patrol during his deployments. He was pretty sure there wouldn't be an IED—improvised explosive device—waiting for him, but situations could be volatile even when there was no shrapnel involved.

He stepped onto the porch and knocked. From inside came the sound of a dog barking and voices, just before the door opened. Fiona stood there looking so beautiful she took his breath away. The sight of her thick, shiny red hair, sweet smile and cute freckled nose was the best thing that happened to him all day. He made a mental note that if Ronan and Keegan made his life miserable for the next few hours, seeing Fiona was worth it. He wished that wasn't the case but he had to be honest.

"Hi. You look pretty—" Before he could say more, a fuzzy, yellow-haired dog nuzzled his hand. He rubbed her head and scratched between her ears.

"This is Duchess. She's a golden retriever, German shepherd mix."

He rubbed a hand over her back. "You look pretty, too."

"Come on in. Everyone's in the kitchen," Fiona said.

He followed her from the spacious living room through a dining room with the table already set for six. Any hope he'd had of dinner with just Fiona and her parents died right there.

The kitchen was big and cozy and loud. Maureen lifted the lid from a large silver pot on the stove. Her husband hovered and sniffed what was cooking, then slid his arms around his wife's waist and kissed her neck.

Seeing the affectionate gesture, their sons groaned loudly.

"Get a room," Ronan teased.

"My eyes," Keegan chimed in. "I can never un-see that."

"I have a room, thank you very much," Paddy retorted.

"And if you don't want to see me kissing your mother, go back to the barn where you belong."

Fiona laughed at the expression on Brendan's face. "I think I've mentioned that they actually live in the converted space. Not that these two couldn't have survived nicely with just stalls, hay and a water trough. What with them being pigs and all."

"Low blow, sis." Ronan walked over and shook Brendan's hand. "Would you like a beer?"

"Thanks." He hadn't expected that nonhostile gesture.

"Wow," Fiona said. "Since when does my big brother have company manners?"

"Always." Maureen put down the big wooden spoon she'd been using and came over to shake his hand. "Welcome, Brendan. I raised all my children to treat visitors to our home with respect. Fiona is teasing."

"No, I'm not, Mom." The sparkle in her eyes said otherwise. "Your manners training didn't bear fruit until I was born. Then Fallon and Brenna imitated my good example. The effort you put in on my two brothers was a complete waste of energy."

Paddy joined the group and shook Brendan's hand. "Hello, son. Glad you could join us."

"My pleasure, sir. Thanks for having me."

"Fiona, can I get you a glass of wine, my fair and favorite sister?" Ronan asked when he brought Brendan the beer bottle.

"I bet you say that to Fallon and Brenna when I'm not around." She shook her head. "And you're not fooling anyone with this Sir Walter Raleigh act. No one here believes you would throw your cloak over a puddle so I wouldn't get my dainty feet wet."

"Maybe Brendan does." Ronan met his gaze but there was no threat, veiled or otherwise.

"I'm staying out of this skirmish."

"Wise man." Ronan nodded. "The thing is, I wouldn't be caught dead in a cloak. It would clash with my cowboy hat. Now, little sister, do you want wine or not?"

"Yes. Thank you."

"I'd like one, too," Maureen said. "Dinner is pretty much ready. But I'm keeping it warm. It would be nice to visit a bit with our guest before we sit down to eat."

Brendan sipped his beer and braced himself. "Visit with our guest" was code for extracting information from him. What were his intentions toward Fiona? Were they friends or more than that? Was he like the jerk who hurt her? He'd tried not to be that guy. And he never let Fiona think he was staying. He'd done his best not to lead her on.

"Are you okay?" Fiona asked, studying him.

"Yes. Why?" He took another drink from his beer bottle then met her gaze.

"I don't know. If I had to describe the look on your face, I'd say it's fight or flight. Like you're waiting for something bad to happen."

"Go ahead. Be honest." Ronan handed his mother and sister stemmed glasses of white wine. "Tell us. We can take it."

As if sensing he needed moral support, Duchess strolled up beside him and nuzzled his fingers. Oddly enough, it helped.

"Okay." The comment fell into the "let's do this man-to-man" category. It was familiar territory for him. "Based on previous experiences, I was expecting hostility from Ronan and Keegan. But this friendliness has thrown me off. Maybe that's the point."

"No." Ronan grinned at his brother. "The point is that Fiona threatened to hurt us if we were mean to you."

"I did not!"

Keegan took up the narrative as if she hadn't spoken. "A man would be a fool not to take her warning to heart." He was doing his best not to laugh.

"You guys are so full of it," she accused them. "Like I could really hurt you."

"They have you on height and weight." Paddy slid an arm across her shoulders and pulled her close for an affectionate hug. "But they are putty in your hands if you shed a tear."

"True." She grinned at Brendan. "It's the nuclear option so I use it on them sparingly."

"When we were kids, she got us in trouble with dad more than once by crying her eyes out," Ronan said.

"I was the first girl after two boys," she explained.

"The little princess," Keegan grumbled.

"And don't think I didn't take full advantage," she gloated. "After Fallon was born it didn't work as well. Then Brenna came along and the boys were just plain outnumbered. I'm pretty sure there was a formal request for surrender when Mom came home from the hospital with another pink-wrapped bundle of joy."

"You call it joy," Ronan said. "I call three little sisters the seventh level of hell."

Brendan happened to be drinking from his beer and almost spit. He started laughing. "Triple the tears."

"No kidding," Keegan agreed. "If only we could send them to a drought-ravaged area where they could do some good."

"Their husbands might object," Maureen pointed out.

"Then just send Fiona." Ronan glanced at his brother who nodded. "No one would miss her."

Brendan would, but kept that to himself. This was a sibling thing and the three of them were very good at it. He wondered what it would have been like to grow up in a big, happy family like this one. It was something a lonely, only child had wanted pretty bad. The Corps was the closest he ever got. Right now he felt as if he was on the outside looking in.

"Stop it, you two," Maureen said. "You talk tough, but you would miss your sister if she wasn't here."

"Yeah," Keegan said. "Like a toothache."

"And yet again, our family happy hour deteriorates into the children fighting," their mother teased. "I think it's time to put dinner on the table."

"I'll give you a hand, sweetheart."

Paddy followed her to the stove, where they filled serving platters and bowls with meat, mashed potatoes, gravy, vegetables and salad. When they thought no one was looking, he dipped his head and kissed his wife full on the mouth.

After years together they were still close.

Brendan had never seen this before. He felt like a fish out of water and couldn't imagine why Fiona had invited him here. She could do so much better than him. The problem was, the idea of her with another man made him crazy. What the hell was he supposed to do?

Fiona stared Brendan down without blinking. She was calling his bluff. "I'll see your ten orange candies and raise you another ten."

He glanced at his cards and shook his head before tossing them on the kitchen table. "A sugar high I can't afford."

"Did you have anything, son?" Paddy asked Brendan.

"No."

"I didn't, either," Fiona said.

"Then it was a good bluff." The older man gave her an approving nod.

Her brothers had left after dinner and they were playing poker with her parents using Halloween candy corn as currency. She was on a roll.

"I like winning," Fiona gloated, raking in her winnings. "Whose deal is it now?"

Paddy stood and stretched. "Not mine. I'm out. I have to get up early in the morning."

Apparently Brendan took that as a sign and got up, too. "I should be going."

Fiona sighed inside. Obviously he had to leave at some point but she wasn't ready for that time to be now. It had been such a fun evening. Her family, even her dork brothers, had warmed to him and he'd loosened up after a while. He seemed to have a good time and the evening went way too fast.

"I'll walk you out," she said.

"Good night, Mrs.—Maureen." He caught himself. Sometime during dinner her parents had given him permission to drop the formality and use their first names. "That was a really good meal."

"You're very welcome, Brendan." Her mom hugged him goodbye. "I hope you'll come back again soon."

"I appreciate that." It wasn't a yes or no and he had a sort of wistful expression on his face. "Thanks again."

He held out his hand to her father. "Paddy. Thank you for having me."

"My pleasure, son."

Brendan headed for the front door and Fiona walked beside him. After he stepped outside on the porch, she joined him and closed the door behind her. The light was on and she could see his brooding expression again.

"I hope you didn't mind my family too much."

"They're great." He met her gaze. "And I was so sure your brothers hated my guts."

"They did." She grinned. "But that wasn't personal. It was just general principle since I'm their sister. They got over it."

"Your parents are nice."

She winced. "'Nice' could mean anything from completely awesome to worse than you could possibly have imagined."

"I meant it in a good way. You're lucky to have them." There was unmistakable envy in his voice.

"I know it." She guessed he was thinking about his own rough childhood, without a mother in the picture. "We play the hand we're dealt. I do wish I could have met your dad."

"He would have liked you."

"And I would have liked him."

"You sound pretty sure about that." He frowned. "How do you know?"

"Because he raised you. Without him you wouldn't be the man you are."

"And what kind of man am I?"

"Kind, brave, honest, hardworking, strong, generous." She smiled at him. "Want me to keep going?"

"Of course." The corners of his mouth slowly turned up.

"Humble, loyal, trustworthy—"

"Stop. Now you're making me blush."

"I mean every word," she said sincerely.

"Fiona—"

His eyes went all intense and he took a half step closer before sliding his arm around her waist, urging her nearer to his body. The heat of him warmed her deep inside and she searched his face, hardly daring to breathe. He touched his mouth to hers, soft and sweet, even as he held her tightly enough that her breasts were crushed to his chest. Their tongues dueled as he kissed her until they were both breathless.

Brendan pulled his mouth away first, but still held her body close. "If I don't go now—"

"I know." But she sighed her disappointment.

"Can I see you tomorrow?" he said against her lips.

"I'd like that." Saying goodbye wasn't nearly so hard when she knew he wanted to see her again soon.

He smiled. "I'll call you."

"Okay. Good night, Brendan."

He lifted a hand in answer, then turned away and left the porch to climb into his truck. Fiona shivered in the cold air and crossed her arms over her chest, refusing to go back inside until his taillights disappeared.

After turning off the living room lights, she passed the dining room table to make sure everything was in order. She walked into the kitchen and was surprised to see her mother still up, hand-washing the big pots she'd used to cook dinner.

Fiona hurried over to the sink. "Mom, let me do those. You go on up to bed."

"I'm almost finished." She set a large lid in the dish drainer on the countertop.

"At least I can dry them," Fiona insisted, grabbing a kitchen towel.

"Thank you, sweetie." They worked side by side in silence for a few moments before her mom said, "I like Brendan. He seems like a very nice young man."

It was always great to have parental approval for one's friends. Just because things had taken an intimate turn didn't mean they were more than that. He'd given her no reason to believe there was anything besides friendship between them.

"He liked you guys, too." She took a large skillet from her mother and started to dry it.

"I'm glad. Your father had very positive things to say and he's a pretty good judge of character."

Fiona had learned the hard way how good her dad was at pegging people. The creep who dumped her had done all the right things when he met her folks, but her dad had seen something that bothered him and could never define exactly what. Turned out he'd been right. So the fact that he was okay with Brendan meant a lot.

"Brendan's not a big talker."

"Nothing wrong with that." Her mom rinsed out the sink. "Gave him more time to look at you."

"What?" Her cheeks grew warm. Why in the world was she blushing? "No, he wasn't."

"I beg to differ. And he wasn't just *looking*, if you know what I mean."

"Actually, I don't." Fiona knew her mother would elaborate. The woman didn't hesitate to share her thoughts.

"It was the *way* he looked at you. There were a lot of feelings in his eyes."

"What kind of feelings?"

"The forever-after kind," Maureen said.

"Oh, please, Mom. You're such a romantic. It's not like that." And she was okay with it. Probably. Maybe.

"Well, I don't know what you think it's like, but that man had the same look in his eyes that your father did just before he said he loved me for the first time."

As much as Fiona wanted to believe that, she couldn't go there. That would take things to a serious place where the potential was really high for getting hurt. Been there, done that. Not again.

"I think you're imagining things."

"Do you, now?" Her mother smiled. "Then answer me

this. Why would he come here to dinner and put himself through the O'Reilly inspection process?"

"He was hungry?"

"I'll admit he showed a healthy appetite, but that's not why."

"I did him a favor." She explained what happened at Ace in the Hole last night.

"I see. You pretended to be his girlfriend so that woman would stop hitting on him." Her mother nodded sagely. "I bet playing that part came real easy to you."

Now that she mentioned it, the role was almost natural. Although she wasn't going to confirm that. "The thing is, he owed me."

"So why did you cash in that marker with a family dinner?"

Leave it to Maureen O'Reilly to get right to the heart of the matter. Fiona wasn't prepared to answer that question because she didn't know the answer for sure. So she asked one of her own.

"When Dad said he loved you, what did you say?"

"That I loved him, too." Her mother's eyes turned soft and glowy at the memory.

"Was it an automatic response? Like something you would say because if you didn't it's like a big thing hanging out there."

"Nothing hung out there," her mother said wryly. "I told him I loved him and it was the honest-to-God truth. I knew it the very first time we met."

Fiona felt a fluttering inside her, the same sensation she'd experienced the first time she saw Brendan. Was there such a thing as love at first sight? Was it hereditary? "How did you know?"

"I wish I could answer, sweetie. I'd be a rich woman because everyone would pay to know that secret. It was

just something that hit me deep down inside, a certainty
that Paddy O'Reilly was the only man who could make
me happy."

"And he has." She had grown up watching them never
miss the chance to touch each other, communicating their
deep love with just a look. Kissing in the kitchen or anywhere else when they thought no one was watching. Or
even when they knew everyone was. "You and Dad have
the absolute perfect relationship."

"Perfect?" There was skepticism in Maureen's voice.
She took the towel from Fiona and folded it, draping the
material over the cupboard door underneath the sink. "Define that."

"You and Dad have set a really high bar for us kids.
It occurs to me that could be why it's taking Ronan and
Keegan so long to settle down."

"And you?"

"I'm resigned to the fact that I'll be a spinster."

Maureen laughed and shook her head. "Let's just clear
something up right now. There's no such thing as a perfect relationship. Marriage is work. Biting your tongue
when you want to be an unreasonable witch. Staying calm
when he's being difficult to deal with."

"That's what I mean," she said. "You and Dad never
fight."

"You never *see* us fight. There's a difference. We made
a promise when Ronan was born to keep our differences
private. But don't mistake that for complete agreement
one hundred percent of the time. Like I said, it's work.
Worth all the effort, but by no means easy."

"Well, you guys sure make it look that way. You're a
very tough act to follow."

"Oh, honey. I know it bothers you that you're turning
thirty and not married like your younger sisters. And I

can't tell you not to let it bother you. That would be a waste of breath and you're entitled to feel any way you want to." Her mother reached out and tucked a lock of hair behind Fiona's ear as if she were still a little girl. "But I can tell you that you're better off alone than marrying the wrong man. A man you don't love. A man who makes you unhappy."

"I know."

"Of course you do. It's just sometimes you can talk yourself into feeling something just because you have a certain goal."

"You're talking about Tate Gibbs, the jackass who left and cheated."

"Yes."

"Are you saying I wasn't in love with him?"

"Only you can answer that, sweetie. I just want you to find someone who makes you as happy as your father does me."

"That's what I want, too," Fiona agreed.

"We've learned that the hallmarks of a good relationship are communication and compromise. It's the hardest work you'll ever do, but it's worth it if both people involved are all in."

"I can see that."

Her mother cupped Fiona's face in her hands. "And I think Brendan wants all in with you."

"Oh, Mom—I can assure you that we are just friends. There's nothing between us." That kiss on the porch might say otherwise, but Fiona was putting on the just-friends face. As far as anyone else knew, that's all they were. It was important everyone believe that because the details of her private life were no one else's business.

"It doesn't matter what I think, just what you do." Maureen kissed her daughter's cheek. "Now, I'm tired. Would you let Duchess out before you go to bed?"

"Sure." She hugged her mom.

"Sleep tight, sweetheart."

"You, too, Mom."

She opened the kitchen door and Duchess ran outside. While waiting for the dog to do her thing, Fiona thought about what her mother said. She wasn't so sure about the forever-after look her mother talked about. Brendan never said anything he didn't mean and he had not said a thing about what they were to each other. Obviously her mother's observation was nothing more than wishful thinking. A hope that they'd get the last O'Reilly daughter married off. Fiona had given up wishing for that.

There was a lot to be said for not wishing your life away and simply living in the moment. And right now she was going to look forward to seeing Brendan tomorrow.

Chapter Twelve

Brendan figured he'd been pretty lucky getting through his deployment unscathed, physically, at least. But surviving an O'Reilly family dinner deserved some kind of medal. The one he gave himself was spending time with Fiona. But no amount of boot camp or survival training could have prepared him for shopping.

Fiona had insisted on meeting him in town at the antiques/thrift store. After she pulled into the lot, he met her at the truck and when she opened the door he said, "Hi."

"Hey." She smiled. "You're punctual."

"Tell me again why we're going to a store that has a bunch of junk. Appliances I can understand, but—"

"I've heard that there are a lot of vintage clothes here and it's a great place to find stuff for a Halloween costume. I still don't have one."

"Are you sure your mom doesn't have some old clothes somewhere?"

She shook her head. "Never even hint in my mother's presence that something she wore is vintage. Just a warning." She shut her door. "If you don't want to do this, I can handle it on my own. I would never want to force you."

He was being a pain in the butt and she should have been annoyed with him, but there wasn't even a hint of irritation in her voice. And that's what made him want to be with her. Even if it meant shopping. He was in shape now, as good as when he'd left the Corps, and could re-enlist anytime he wanted. It was coming up on "fish or cut bait" time and the pretty redhead with the sunny disposition wasn't making the decision easy.

"Let's roll," he said.

They walked around to the front door, under a sign that said, Everything Old. On either side were half-barrel planters, baskets of stick-in-the-ground garden decorations and an old horse-drawn plow.

He pointed it out. "What would anyone want with that?"

Fiona thought for a moment. "With a little paint that could be a lawn decoration for Sunshine Farm." She looked up at him. "One man's trash is another man's treasure. You should know that better than anyone since you're a genius at fixing stuff—new and old."

"I can't tell whether I was just complimented or smacked down."

"Maybe both." She grinned. "Now man up, Tanner. We're going in."

"I've got your six."

"My what now?"

"Your back." Except his gaze dropped to her curvy and spectacular butt when she preceded him through the doorway.

The interior was a lot bigger than it looked from the outside and separated into individual booths containing everything from old furniture to glassware and small appliances. In two seconds he realized this wouldn't be a quick in-and-out.

A woman walked up to them and smiled. She was a pretty brunette, somewhere in her twenties, with big turquoise eyes and freckles on her nose.

"Hi, I'm Geneva Quinn. Welcome to Everything Old."

Fiona held out her hand. "Fiona O'Reilly. This is Brendan Tanner. I haven't seen you around. Are you new to Rust Creek Falls?"

"Yeah. And you haven't seen me because I've been working a lot of hours putting my business together."

"I love what you've done with the place." Fiona looked up at him. "There was a flood in Rust Creek Falls in 2013. Half the town was under water, homes were unlivable and people abandoned them. We went through some hard times. There was a business here but it didn't survive. It's been empty until now."

"I'm getting a break on the cost and renting out space to anyone who has merchandise to sell."

"Are there any spaces available?" Brendan wondered. "I'm asking for a friend." Luke might be interested, even though Brendan probably wouldn't be around to see whether it worked out.

"Have them come see me. Meanwhile, have fun browsing."

"We will." Fiona looked at Brendan and whatever she saw made her smile. "Brendan can't wait to get started."

"I can see that," the other woman said wryly. "But he's here and he's cute. What more could you ask from a boyfriend?"

"He's not my boyfriend," she said fairly firmly. "Just a friend."

Then Fiona took off and turned left to start shopping. He caught up with her halfway down the aisle.

"So who do you know looking to rent a space here?" she asked.

"Luke mentioned something about it. Possibly another revenue source for his foundation." If there was a God, she would not ask more questions.

"And what is he planning to sell in a booth?" She walked into a space to check out a framed picture hanging on the wall.

"He said something about donations."

"Would these donations be things that you are able to fix?" She glanced over her shoulder at him.

"The man is relentless." He knew the subtext of her question was about him sticking around and that was something he couldn't answer.

She didn't ask anything but continued perusing booths till she found a rack of old clothes—hats, shoes, an old fur coat. She meticulously looked at all the hanging items but didn't see what she wanted.

Brendan already knew what he wanted. Fiona. Every time their shoulders brushed or hands bumped, he wanted to take her in his arms and kiss her until she made those breathy little moaning noises.

"I'm going in here," she said as something in a booth caught her eye.

"Okay." He followed her. "This is your op. I'm just here to look cute."

"Mission accomplished." She gave him a flirty look, then turned her attention to a stack of clothes.

Brendan scanned the shelves holding plates, glasses, pots and pans. In a corner of the booth he saw a shelf of toys and walked over to check them out. Trucks and cars were lined up haphazardly. In the back, almost hidden by action figures, he saw a military vehicle painted in jungle camouflage. He reached past the clutter and picked it up. His stomach knotted when he realized it was an awful lot like the one his mom gave him when he was five.

"Brendan?" Fiona put her hand on his arm. "Did you hear me? Are you okay?"

Apparently she'd said something and he didn't hear because of the roaring in his ears. "I'm fine."

Her gaze narrowed. "You can talk to me."

Because that's what friends did. She'd said that before. He knew the stubborn look on her face better now and she wasn't going to let this drop. Looking at the toy in his hand was like a glimpse into the past, a place he never wanted to visit again.

"I had one of these when I was a kid." He stared at the thing. "My mother gave it to me when she broke the news she was leaving."

"Oh, Brendan—" She sighed. "Of all the memories you could have found here, why did it have to be that one?"

"Yeah. What are the odds?" He'd already told her a boatload of bad stuff, but there was more and it came bubbling up. "It took a while, but my dad moved on. He let another woman into his life."

"Good."

"I guess." Leon had been happy. She was nice and they were like a family for a while. "But she left, too."

Fiona pressed her lips together for a moment. "That just bites."

"More than you know." He almost laughed. Most people would have given the stock "I'm sorry" or something equally as useless. She told it like it was.

"What aren't you telling me?"

"I had already committed to the Marines when she dumped him. I couldn't stick around and he was alone to deal with it. In a short span he lost two people he cared about. Double whammy."

"I'm sure he understood why you had to go," she said.

"Yeah. But I know it was that much harder for him." He looked at her then, the sympathy in her eyes.

"He didn't lose you, Brendan. Children grow up and leave home—" She stopped as her words sank in. "Well, not me and my brothers. It's different with the ranch. But letting kids be independent is the natural order of things."

"I know. It's just when he got sick—"

"You felt bad that you didn't spend more time with him when you could have."

He nodded, a lump in his throat as he replaced the toy on the shelf. "If we could see the future, a decision today would be a lot easier."

She moved close and wrapped her arms around his waist, resting her cheek on his chest. "I hear it in your voice. You feel as if you left a man behind, and I know marines take pride in not doing that. But I believe if your dad was here, he would say that he was glad you found a career that fulfilled you. If leaving him was part of that, so be it. If you were happy, he was happy."

Maybe it was the hug or just the right words at the right time, but he felt as if a weight lifted from his heart. As if he'd received absolution. Somehow he knew in his soul that she was right.

"Thank you," he whispered against her hair. "That helps."

"You're welcome." She hugged him tight for a moment, then backed away and smiled. "If I was a shrink that would cost you big."

"Oh? So what do I owe you?"

"Takeout from Ace in the Hole. We'll eat it at your place."

There was a little bit of a bad girl glint in her eyes and he had a sneaking suspicion about what she had in mind at his place. "Count me in."

* * *

Fiona knew exactly what her "fee" entailed and it wasn't just dinner to go. Ace in the Hole was their first stop. Together they walked inside, up to the bar and sat side by side on a couple of stools. The place was a lot busier than she'd hoped.

She wanted to be in Brendan's arms desperately and was pretty sure he was impatient to have her there. But she knew getting to his cabin discreetly was going to be a challenge. It wasn't that she was ashamed of being with him. She just didn't want everyone in town to know about it.

He was basically another stranger. Unlike the last one, he didn't lead her on. But when he left she didn't want to be the talk of the town again. That much humiliation was enough for a lifetime. No one would pity her if they didn't know she and Brendan were a thing.

So the problem at a crowded Ace in the Hole was how to get food to go without anyone asking questions and putting two and two together. Because her, him, his bed—it was going to happen.

Rosey was helping out behind the bar and walked over to them. "Brendan. Fiona. Nice to see you again. This is getting to be a habit."

The woman was fishing for information and Fiona was going to give her as little as possible. "I wouldn't say that. We checked out that new place, Everything Old, for stuff to put together a Halloween costume and—"

"You two coordinating costumes for Luke and Eva's party?"

"We were just browsing," Brendan said evasively.

Fiona needed to lay down a distraction. "By the way, I don't know if you heard that Luke is making the party a fund-raiser for the foundation he's starting. His goal is to fix up some of the Sunshine Farms cabins and build more for veterans who need a place to decompress and adjust to civilian life after deployment or leaving the military."

"I hadn't heard. And you had me at 'fund-raiser,'" Rosey said. "But that's a real good thing he's doing. I know Sam will be on board."

Fiona nodded, pleased that the other woman's attention had been diverted from speculation about her and Brendan. "I knew you would get it. Luke would be grateful if you could spread the word. And if anyone can't be there but wants to donate, he's got a website. The information will be in the *Gazette*."

"Happy to help." She met Brendan's gaze and nodded. "Now, what can I get you two?"

"What else? Burgers and fries." Brendan looked at Fiona and added, "To go."

His tone was übercasual but instantly there was an elephant in the room. Rosey's eyes gleamed with curiosity although she didn't say anything.

Fiona felt the need to fill the silence and said the first thing that popped into her mind. "It's crowded in here tonight. So we're going to take the food to my house and watch TV."

"Uh-huh." The look on the other woman's face said she didn't buy that for a second. "Since when does Maureen O'Reilly let anyone come into her house and eat food she didn't cook for them?"

"I just didn't want to bother her and make a mess in the kitchen after dinner."

"Fiona Kathleen O'Reilly, your nose is growing with every word that comes out of your mouth."

No one used all three of her names unless she was in trouble. "I'm sensing some skepticism—"

Rosey put her hands on her ample hips and had a look on

her face that would intimidate even the most interrogation-hardened soldier.

"Okay," she said. "Would you believe a picnic?"

"It's cold and dark outside. Do I look like I was born yesterday?" The older woman held up a hand. "Don't answer that."

Fiona gave Brendan an exasperated look. "Bail me out here. Say something."

"On it." He met the bar owner's gaze. "We're taking food back to my cabin at Sunshine Farm. After I feed her, she's going to have her way with me."

"Brendan!"

"What?" He looked unapologetic and self-satisfied. "It's the truth. This scenario doesn't leave much latitude for a believable lie."

"Still, you were a marine. I expected you to put some effort into coming up with a good cover story."

"Fiona—" Rosey reached over and patted her hand. "Honey, it's not like I didn't know the minute I saw you two."

"Why? What gave it away? Is it written on my forehead?" she demanded. "'Getting lucky tonight'?"

Rosey shrugged. "It's clear that you're determined to keep it private. I respect that. And I have a reputation to maintain. Someone tells me something while I'm behind this bar, I keep it to myself. Like attorney-client privilege." She was dead serious. "This information goes no further."

"Thanks, Rosey."

"Okay. So, burgers and fries coming right up." She turned away and headed into the back.

Brendan swiveled his stool toward her, then moved hers so that she was facing him. The only parts of their bodies touching were their knees, but she felt him all over. She sensed he wanted to take her hand, but he didn't.

"I'm sorry," he said.

"It's not your fault I suck at lying."

He smiled. It was so loud in the place that no one could hear when he said, "I really want to touch you right now."

She wanted him to. Badly.

"I'm glad you're a bad liar," he told her. "In my humble opinion, it's one of your very best qualities."

"You think I'm silly, but this town—" She rested her arm on the bar beside them. "Everyone talks and I don't want it to be about me."

Not again.

He touched her hand, just a friendly gesture to anyone who might see. "For what it's worth, I think Rosey was being honest. She won't spread anything about us."

"This place is packed." She looked around at the crowd. "Someone is bound to see that we're leaving with food."

"Even so, that could mean anything," he said. "We could be taking it to your place to watch TV."

She shook her head. "Everyone will come to the same conclusion Rosey did. My mom feeds anyone who comes over. She's got an extra refrigerator and freezer jammed with enough food to feed a small country."

"I'm sorry," he said with a sigh. "But I've been eating meals with Eva and Luke. Or they send leftovers to me. There's a small microwave and compact fridge in the place. But I haven't stocked up on supplies."

Traveling light, she thought, *because that makes it easier to take off.* He was deliberately not putting down roots. She felt a twinge of something in her chest and consciously chose to ignore it. Every moment she spent with him was a memory to pull out on a cold, lonely winter night. Maybe it was stupid, but that was all the more reason she hoped Rosey kept her promise.

"It's okay," she said.

"No." He looked down for a moment before meeting her gaze. "And if you want me to go home now, I'll take you back to your truck."

Fiona met his gaze as her inner voice firmly said "no way" to that suggestion. This was like writing a free-lance article. When an opportunity came along you took it because it might not happen again. If sex was all she wanted, prospects were abundant. But she was old-fashioned and needed to have feelings. It didn't have to be love, but she had to like and respect a man to go to bed with him. Brendan fit those criteria and then some. Her only concern was caring too much.

She shook her head. "You promised me food. And I've been told that you always keep your promises. But if I didn't know better, I'd say you're trying to get out of this."

"Oh, honey—" A slow, sexy smile turned up the corners of his mouth while his eyes caught fire. "If we weren't trying to fly under the radar I'd show you here and now just how committed I am to keeping my word."

"Okay, then." Desire flared inside her. "When our food comes, we'll—"

Rosey came out of the back just then with a large brown bag in her hand. She set it in front of them. "Order up."

"You wouldn't happen to have a bottle of wine I could buy," Brendan asked, "would you?"

"I can damn sure find one," Rosey said. "This is a bar, for Pete's sake."

"And would I be pushing my luck to talk you out of a couple of glasses?"

"Do I look like a miracle worker?" she said in mock

annoyance. Then she grinned. "You're my kind of man, Brendan Tanner. If I were younger and—"

"Not married?" Fiona said.

"That, too. I am partial to military types, as you both already know. And I'm not fooling anyone. Sam Traven is the love of my life."

"You just broke my heart," Brendan teased.

"There seems to be an epidemic of nose growing in here tonight." She laughed. "I'll get that wine and some glasses for you."

Fiona stared at him. "How are we supposed to get all of that out of here without attracting attention?"

"Leave that to a marine."

When the bar owner came back with another bag, Brendan leaned over and whispered in the older woman's ear. Rosey grinned and nodded.

In a low voice he said to Fiona, "Get ready to make a run for it."

"Really? Because us sprinting out of here with two big bags won't be noticeable at all."

"I didn't mean literally. Just wait for the signal," he instructed.

"How will I know what it is?"

"Trust me. You'll know."

A few moments later, from the other end of the bar, Rosey tapped a spoon against a wineglass to get the attention of everyone in the room. "It's awful darn close to Halloween. Let's call this trick or treat. Everyone gets a drink on the house. Come on up here and tell me what you're having."

There was a swelling of noise—voices, cheers and chairs scraping as everyone stood. En masse, people headed to the end of the bar.

Brendan grabbed the two brown bags and slid off the stool. "Now."

Fiona followed his lead and they walked out the door. She glanced back to scope out their escape. Not one person noticed them. They were all focused on getting a drink order in to Rosey.

When they reached his truck in the parking lot she said, "You, sir, have skills."

"And an impressive bar tab now." He set the bags on the floor in the back, then grinned at her. The flashing neon beer sign in the bar's window highlighted the sexy gleam in his eyes. "But you haven't seen anything yet."

She whispered to herself, "Be still my heart."

But that was an impossible order to obey. Her heart was about to jump out of her chest. Her stomach was growling, but her hormones were stirred up, signaling a hunger that went a whole lot deeper. This was something that would feed her soul.

He'd gone the extra mile of getting wine and glasses. She couldn't wait until his attention to detail was focused on her.

Chapter Thirteen

Brendan parked his truck behind the cabin and turned off the headlights. He'd never wanted a woman as badly as he wanted Fiona right now but she wanted this to be under the radar. The quicker he got them inside, the faster he could have her.

"I'll go first and take the food. You wait here and if I run into anyone, I'll get rid of them as fast as I can. Then you advance, hugging the wall. I'll leave the door partly open."

"Roger that."

"I think you're enjoying this," he said.

"Maybe a little."

He grinned, then opened his door and got out. Fiona did the same, coming around to stand beside him. The scent of her skin drifted to him and stoked the fire he'd been trying and failing to bank since she suggested take-out at his place.

"Let's do this," he said.

He grabbed the two bags from the rear seat and walked the path between cabins. There were lights on next door, but he got to the front, and the newest Sunshine Farm resident was nowhere to be seen.

Rounding the corner, he stepped on the porch, went inside and set the bags on the small table before turning on the light. Moments later Fiona slipped through the door and closed it behind her.

"I don't think anyone saw me."

Brendan had a question about why she was so intent on keeping this a secret, but he was too hungry to ask. Starving for food—and for her.

He pulled the bottle of wine from the bag along with the glasses. There was a corkscrew with a note from Rosey. It said: *This is a loaner. You're welcome.*

He owed that woman big-time.

While he opened the bottle and poured each of them a glass, Fiona removed burgers and fries from the bag and put the food in the small countertop microwave to warm.

Brendan got out plates and when everything was reheated, they sat down to eat. He'd been here at Sunshine Farm for almost two months and this was the first time he'd had a meal with anyone in this cabin. It was so damn normal and ordinary that an odd sort of loneliness bled into him. Who else could be lonely with a beautiful woman sitting across from him? Wouldn't be the first time it occurred to him that he needed to have his head examined.

After all, he was here with Fiona. He probably shouldn't be but there was a part of him that felt if he didn't have her he would implode.

It didn't take them long to wolf down the food. Then Fiona got up and cleared away the paper and bags. Brendan refilled their wineglasses. She came back to the table and stood close enough for him to feel the heat of her body, just enough to make his pulse race faster and his heart pound even harder. There was a sweet, small-town innocence about her that was irresistible. And he had to ask one more time.

"Are you okay with this, Fiona?"

"It was my idea, remember?" She smiled a little shyly. "I wanted to be with you again so much. But I was afraid you didn't want me."

"You are so wrong about that."

He took her face in his hands and kissed her. She opened her mouth and he eagerly dipped his tongue inside. She tasted of burger, wine and willingness. As he explored, a soft, pleading moan vibrated in her throat. The breathy, sexy sound fired up his blood like a lightning strike to dry brush.

One moment he was kissing her, and the next they were tugging at each other's clothes, yanking off boots, discarding shirts, jeans, underwear, leaving a trail all the way to his bed. He yanked down the spread and tumbled her onto the mattress. She laughed happily and opened her arms to him. Didn't have to ask him twice. He joined her and pulled her close, savoring the feel of her bare skin against his.

"You're so soft," he whispered against her neck.

"And you're not." Her hands went up and down his back as she nestled her breasts to his chest.

Brendan moved away, just far enough so that he could hold a breast in his palm. He looked into her passion-glazed eyes and whispered, "Tell me what you want."

"Only you."

She cupped his cheek in her hand and he was lost. He touched her everywhere and she had her way with him. Finally he couldn't stand it another second and opened the nightstand, groping for a condom. He found one and put it on. Then he rolled her onto her back and she opened to him. Taking great care, he entered her and felt her sigh.

He moved slowly, listening to her shallow breathing, waiting for a sign that she was on the edge. Then he felt her hands on his back, the almost frantic movement, and her hips arched upward, demanding more of him. He thrust deeper and faster until she cried out and clung to him, saying his name over and over.

When she nuzzled his chest and spread soft kisses on his collarbone, he started to move again. She met him, thrust for thrust, pulling him deeper as she wrapped her legs around his hips. He went higher, overdosing on the sight, sound and feel of her before light exploded behind his eyes and pleasure roared through him, leaving heat everywhere. Judging from her throaty moans, he'd brought her to another orgasm.

He held her tightly against him while their breathing slowed to something resembling normal and he could actually think again. Even then they didn't move for a while. Finally he left her just long enough to go into the bathroom and dispose of the condom. It was a weird feeling, but he couldn't shake it, as if she wouldn't be there when he got back. But she was and he slid into bed, pulling her close to his side.

She rested her cheek on his chest. "So, those skills you were bragging about..."

"Yes?"

"You didn't lie." Her voice was dreamy, satisfied.

Contentment filled him, something he wasn't sure he'd ever felt before. Something he didn't trust and shouldn't get used to. "It's not bragging if it's true. And I always do my best to tell the truth."

"It's a very good quality," she agreed. "What are some of your other character strengths?"

"Well..." He thought about that and visions of his dad popped into his mind. "Leon's life lessons."

"Care to share?"

"My dad was a drill sergeant before I knew what one was. He was always saying, 'Don't slouch. Stand up straight. Never lie, steal or cheat.' And he made sure I knew that there are a lot of ways to do all three."

"Such as?"

"Promising to love and cherish, for better or worse. Don't say it unless you mean it."

"So his life lessons were about your mom walking out," she said.

"Yeah." He held her just a little tighter.

"You know, I have no idea what it feels like to grow up without a mother. I'm trying to play devil's advocate, not be patronizing. And it will never make you feel better about what happened."

Brendan couldn't help but smile at the way she was qualifying whatever it was she planned to say. "Just spill it."

"A lot of kids don't have either parent. They're orphans or abandoned. At least you had a loving father."

"That's almost harder for me. He was a great dad—wise and supportive. And he never had anyone love him back the way he deserved."

"You loved him," she pointed out.

"It's not the same." He wrapped her hand in his and settled both on his chest. "I mean a personal adult relationship."

"That's not your fault."

"Maybe it is." He absently brushed his other thumb over her shoulder. "What if my mother left because of me?"

"What? You were five."

"And a typical boy—loud and physical. Maybe I made her nuts and she couldn't take it."

"Correct me if I'm wrong, but didn't you tell me she said your dad was good-looking but she needed more excitement?"

Brendan could still remember his mother's voice and the words. Her telling him he would be better off with just his dad. "That's what she said."

"If you never believe me about anything, believe this. She left for her own selfish reasons and it had nothing to do with you. In fact, a woman like that probably did you and your dad a favor."

Brendan recalled his dad telling him the same thing, but he didn't buy it. Somehow Fiona saying it struck just the right chord because the knot of guilt inside him seemed to unravel.

"It was her loss," Fiona added.

"Understood."

"Really?" She tipped her face up to study him. "You're not going to tell me I'm wrong?"

"Not when you're right. There's that whole 'telling the truth' thing."

"Wow." She threw her arm over his abdomen and snuggled closer. "The only thing that makes me happier than being right is you trusting me enough to share all this."

He wasn't sure why he had. Maybe it just got too heavy to carry by himself. Or his glimpse into nice and normal had him going soft. Either way, he didn't regret talking about it.

"Glad you're happy." He kissed her forehead. "Especially since the trip to Everything Old was a failure."

"I'll come up with something for a costume. My sisters will help."

Brendan envied her having people to fall back on. Now that his dad was gone he didn't have that. Unless he reenlisted.

"Speaking of Halloween," she said, "the party/fund-raiser is coming up."

"Yeah."

"I was wondering if maybe—" she met his gaze "—you'd want to go with me."

"You mean a date?"

"Sort of, I guess. My family will be there and quite a few people from town."

That made him wonder again. "So it would be very public."

"Yeah."

"Then why did we jump through hoops at Ace in the Hole to keep anyone from knowing about us?"

"I— It's just—" She tensed and slid away. "That was different."

"How?" He missed feeling her bare skin against his. More important right now was that he was missing her point.

"It's no one else's business what I do and everyone would have jumped to the conclusion that we were going to sleep together."

Some survival instinct told him not to point out that they had slept together and were still in his bed. "But if we show up at the party together, won't they jump to that conclusion?"

"I never claimed it was rational. You don't know what it's like to be the talk of the town. And not in a good way. Everyone has an opinion and they share it with you, to your face. It's awful. The pity is hard enough, but the worst was when someone said I should have known better. And they were right." She sat up and pulled the sheet with her, covering her breasts. "It was humiliating and something I never want to experience again. So tonight I jumped through hoops because I didn't want to be town topic number one tomorrow. I didn't want it to be common knowledge that I'm sleeping with you."

And he would rather die than have her humiliated—especially because of him. He was trained to protect. It was part of who he was, the best part. "Understood."

"Okay. So I guess what I just said is that it's not you. It's me."

"Roger that."

She nodded and gave him a small smile. "I don't think it's a problem being seen together at the party. We're friends. We could meet there. What do you think?"

He thought until right this moment he'd been leaning toward staying in Rust Creek Falls. Then she asked him to the party and he realized she was starting to have expectations. He was damaged goods and couldn't give her what she needed. And it killed him that he couldn't. On top of that, he prided himself on the truth but he'd been lying to himself.

He'd drawn a line in the sand with her and crossed it anyway. Giving in just one more time tonight hadn't felt like a big deal until now, and this was where he paid the price for his mistake. She might think that keeping them a secret was protecting her, but she was wrong. Whether she knew it or not, she wanted more than he could give. So it had to stop or she would get hurt; he would do anything to keep that from happening. Putting off his decision had been selfish but it wasn't just about what was best for him any longer. And suddenly his mind was made up. He knew what he had to do.

Do it quick. Rip off the Band-Aid. Tell her the truth.

"I don't think it's a good idea for me to meet you there."

"Why?"

"I have to be honest, Fiona. I plan to reenlist in the Marine Corps. It's where I belong."

"I didn't realize you'd made up your mind. I thought you were going to stay." Her eyes grew wide—and there was a bruised look in them. "I could have sworn you belonged here. The whole town embraced you. And your business—"

"That's Luke's idea, not mine," he said. "When I came to Sunshine Farm it was to clear my head, figure out my next move. Mission accomplished. The fact is I shouldn't have brought you here tonight. I'm—"

"Don't you dare say you're sorry," she warned. The bruised look turned to betrayal, as if she couldn't stand the sight of him. "I knew what I was getting into, what I wanted. And now I want to go home."

As much as he didn't want to let her go, Brendan wouldn't try to change her mind. It was for the best. He'd already made more mistakes with her than he wanted to admit. But telling her the truth about his decision to re-enlist wasn't one of them. In fact, now that he knew the depth of the pain she'd suffered being the target of town gossip, he was absolutely sure this was the right thing. Protecting her made him feel good.

Was that selfish? He was really afraid that leaving her made him just like his mother.

Fiona dumped another bunch of dirty hay into the wheelbarrow. Shoveling crap seemed like an appropriate job the day after Brendan told her he was reenlisting. Which was just a noble way of saying "leaving." She'd known it was a possibility, but that hadn't stopped her from falling in love with him. She hadn't wanted to face her growing feelings but that didn't make it any less true. Or her pain any less real. Maybe deep down she'd believed he wouldn't go. That he would want to stay. For her. And if she'd acknowledged sooner that she loved him, would she feel any less stupid and foolish?

That brought a fresh wave of pain and more tears. It was a good thing scooping up muck wasn't a precision job because her vision was blurry.

"Hey, Fee." Ronan walked into the stall behind her. "Have you seen my wire cutters?"

"No." It was an effort to keep her voice even and normal but she was pretty sure she pulled it off. She also kept her back to him.

"Are you sure? I know you've seen them. The ones with the yellow handles you're always nagging me to put back where they belong."

"I've seen them, but it's not actually my responsibility to watch them. And if you'd taken my advice you wouldn't be bugging me now."

"Wow, someone got up on the wrong side of the bed."

There was no right side when you got out of the wrong bed. "Go away."

"Not until you tell me where to look for the wire cutters."

"Why would I have any idea where you left them? I don't know everything—"

"Fiona?" He circled around to face her. "What's wrong?"

"You can't find that stupid tool, that's what." She rubbed a flannel-covered arm over her face.

"Are you crying?"

"No." She turned away.

"So you're just in a crap mood for no reason?" Her brother sounded skeptical.

She was angry and hurt. That tended to put a dent in a girl's normally sunny disposition. "Aren't I allowed to be crabby? Everyone else in this family gets to. Why not me?"

"Because you're Fiona. The cheerful one who is always happy to lend a hand. The one who moves heaven and earth to help find the lost wire cutters. That's why we all come to you."

"Everyone comes to me for everything." Tears were rolling down her cheeks and if he saw, he wouldn't go away. And she really, really wanted him to. "The truth is I don't know where everything is. I can't fix anything. I'm an idiot—"

He moved around and in front of her. "I knew it. You are crying."

"Give the man a silver belt buckle. Now would you please go away?" She put one hand over her face. The other one held the shovel.

He took the tool from her and put it down. Then she felt his arms come around her. "Don't cry, Fee."

"What if I want to?"

"Then go for it." He rubbed her back.

"I hate crying. I'm not a crier."

"Then don't," he said patiently.

"I c-can't help it."

"Okay, then. You just do whatever the hell you want."

"I don't need your permission," she snapped.

"Got that right." He gave her a squeeze, then stepped back, hands on her upper arms as he met her gaze. "But do you want to tell me who you're really mad at?"

"No."

"Well, I'm not leaving until you do. This is me. The brother who's there to hold you when you cry." He let her go and blew out a long breath. "But I have to say this is creeping me out. It's just wrong. You falling apart. I've never seen you like this. Not even when you found out that bozo lied and cheated on you."

That's because she wasn't in love with the bozo. She'd

been upset because he'd publicly humiliated her, but there was never any soul-deep pain. Not like this.

"It's nothing, Ronan. Don't worry your pretty little head. Just let me finish mucking out the stalls. Then I have an article to work on—"

"I want a name. Tell me who's responsible for making you cry so I can beat him up."

In spite of her misery, that made her laugh. Her brother was a big guy and in really good shape because ranching was hard, physical work. But Brendan had warrior skills. He'd been trained.

"What's so funny?" Ronan held up a hand. "Don't get me wrong. I'm not sorry the blubbering stopped, but what did I say?"

"I wouldn't advise a confrontation. He probably knows three hundred ways to incapacitate a man with one arm tied behind his back."

"I knew it!" He glared, not at her, just in general. "Tanner. And I warned that bastard, too."

And he'd warned her, but she'd been so sure her feelings could be controlled. Because Brendan was another stranger who was leaving and she wouldn't be stupid again. No, it wasn't her. Love was stupid.

"It's not his fault, Ronan."

"He's the one who made you cry," her brother said angrily. "By definition that makes it his fault."

"You don't even know what's going on."

"Because you won't tell me. If I have to, I'll go get answers from him—"

"No!" Fiona didn't miss the intensity in her brother's blue eyes and could practically see testosterone churning through him. He was looking for retribution on her behalf and she loved him so much for that. But sometimes things weren't meant to be, and this thing with her and

Brendan was one of those times. It would be so much easier if someone was at fault but that wasn't the case.

"Tell me why I shouldn't give him a piece of my mind." He pointed at her, a warning expression on his face. "And don't you dare say it's because I can't spare it."

That coaxed a small smile from her, but almost instantly it faded. "He's leaving—reenlisting in the Marines."

"Oh." Ronan looked deflated, as if someone punctured his indignation balloon. "Why would he go back?"

"A lot of reasons." She thought for a moment and made the decision to reveal some of the personal things Brendan had told her. She wasn't sure why, but it was important that Ronan not hate him. "He never wanted to leave the military in the first place."

"Then why did he?"

She told him about his father.

Ronan nodded his understanding. "Tough break. Can't imagine losing Dad. Or Mom."

Fiona couldn't, either, and didn't even want to think about it. "Speaking of that… His father was a single dad and they were particularly close because of it. But Brendan really loved his career, the guys he served with. It was the place he felt he belonged."

She'd been so sure he was fitting into the Rust Creek Falls community. In her heart, hope had taken hold, along with deeper feelings. So the reenlistment news came as a shock. A deeply painful one.

Last night, when she told him she wanted to go home, he'd brought her back to town to get her truck. On the drive they'd hardly said two words to each other. Although he'd made progress being conversational, Brendan wasn't naturally talkative. From him silence wasn't a surprise. Her excuse was being numb. That wore off this morning and she really missed feeling nothing. Now she felt heartsick and it sucked.

"Well, damn it." Ronan rubbed a hand across his neck, a gesture of frustration because there was no one to focus his anger on.

"I know. It's a little hard on a girl's ego to find out she just wasn't enough for him to stay—" Emotion choked off the rest of what she'd been about to say.

"So you really care about him?"

She nodded because she still couldn't get a single word past the lump in her throat.

"If it's any consolation, I don't think he set out to hurt you. I think he probably did his best not to."

"Yeah." She pressed her lips together for a moment. "I knew he was another stranger in town who was leaving, but then I got to know him. He's nothing like the bozo. Brendan is a good man. I didn't plan on this. My eyes were wide-open." She shrugged. "It just sort of happened in spite of me."

"I'd still like to beat him up," Ronan muttered.

"Because you'd feel better if he cleaned your clock?" *Men* are *from Mars*, she thought.

"Pain is easy. But watching my sister hurting and not being able to take it away is hard." He looked almost as miserable as she felt.

"You're going to make me cry again." She sniffled. "Stop being so sweet."

"Okay." He looked down for a moment, and then the corners of his mouth turned up. "So, now will you tell me where my wire cutters are?"

"Seriously?" Playfully, she slugged him in the arm, then threw her arms around him in a hug. "Don't worry about me. I'll be fine. This too shall pass. I'll get over it."

"I know you will. O'Reillys are made of stern stuff. We might bend but we don't break."

"Now go away and let me finish my work," she said.

"Okay. Maybe Keegan has been into my tools again and I can kick his ass."

Fiona laughed as she shooed her brother away. But after he was gone she felt even more alone. What he'd said about the O'Reillys being tough must have been true, because it surprised her that she'd been able to put on a brave front. The thing was that talking it out with her brother had made her realize the awful truth.

She would go on, but now there was an emptiness inside her that could never be filled. Her heart wasn't just broken. It was shattered and would never be whole enough to love again.

Chapter Fourteen

Brendan would give anything if he could forget the look in Fiona's eyes when she got out of his truck last night. He recognized betrayal and pain. Hurting her was the last thing he wanted to do. Some hero he was. It was putting off the inevitable, but he wished she hadn't asked him to go to the party. With her family there, no less. But when she did, he knew he had to reenlist and she needed to know. So he told her his decision and now she hated him. Damn it.

Now he was in the barn workshop at the crack of dawn trying to repair an electric frying pan because he couldn't sleep. Might as well do something until he had to be at Jamie Stockton's place to take a look at his baler. The pan fix wasn't going well. He'd taken it apart and was looking for something obvious. A loose connection.

It's almost always in the wiring. His dad had told him to start there every time.

Maybe his own wiring needed a fix, Brendan thought, since he was so screwed up. He'd been completely sincere when he told Fiona she was better off without him. He would just hurt her again and he couldn't stand that.

But more unbearable was the thought of her with someone else. That was a classic example of being screwed up.

"Knock, knock."

Brendan turned at the sound of Luke's voice. His friend
was standing in the shop doorway. "Hey. You don't need
an invitation. This is your barn."

"Yeah." The other man walked closer and stopped beside the bench, which was covered with tools and broken-
down appliances. "But you made this shop yours. Breathed
life into a room full of dust and cobwebs."

"You're giving me too much credit."

"I disagree." He glanced at the small appliances, bat-
tered power tools and even bikes that were lined up to
be looked at. "If this space was mine, that stuff would
just be junk. From where I'm standing it looks like proof
that folks around here believe you can fix them. They're
counting on you."

Except for his dad, no one had depended on him since
he left the Marine Corps. "Are you here to try to talk me
into opening a shop again?"

"No, actually." Luke's expression was deadly serious.
"I came to ask when you decided to reenlist."

"How did you—"

"It's a small town. News travels fast. That's both good
and bad." The other man shrugged.

Brendan hadn't told anyone except… "You talked to
Fiona."

"No. Her brother Ronan. Apparently she was upset.
He dragged the information out of her."

Brendan winced even though the other man's voice
was calm, not critical. When did this stopover in Rust
Creek Falls get more complicated than him figuring out
his next move? Stupid question, because he knew the

answer. The moment he saw Fiona. She complicated the hell out of his life.

Then Luke's words sank in. She hadn't shared his plan willingly but had been too upset to hide her feelings. Her brother out-stubborned her and Brendan had to admire that, and the family. Seems she wasn't the only one who cared; she came from a long line of people who believed in compassion and commitment. That was something he'd been looking for all his life.

It was why he was returning to the Corps, the one place he was guaranteed to fit.

He didn't answer Luke's question about when he'd made up his mind, but braced himself for a hard sell. At the same time he couldn't help wondering why this guy would waste his time and energy.

"Look, Luke, I don't mean to sound ungrateful. I appreciate you giving me a place to clear my head, get in shape and figure things out." He faced the other man straight on. "I've done that. Now I'm ready—"

"Not so fast." His friend held up a hand. "Hear me out."

"You can't talk me out of it. This is the right thing." But an image of Fiona flashed into his mind, running in here with her cheeks flushed and her red hair flying. She was his passion and his pain. That realization took some of the intensity out of him.

"I'm not trying to talk you out of anything," Luke said. "I just want to tell you a story."

This was starting to grate. "I'm not a kid—"

"It's my story," the other man said. "And I think you owe me a listen."

So he was calling in a marker. Brendan folded his arms over his chest. This man had a great piece of property and was putting it to good use. His family was here, he had a wife who loved him and everyone in town respected him for his commitment to give back to the community. So what was his deal?

"Okay. I'll listen. But I'm just not sure what Mr. Perfect can say that will change my mind."

"I'm not perfect. Not by a long shot." Luke laughed but the sound was mocking. "I have so much to make up for."

"No way."

Luke gave him a look, then started talking. "I was wild and willful when I was younger. When you're the oldest of seven, you're expected to set an example. But that's not what I did. At best my behavior could be described as a horrible warning. I was young and stupid."

Brendan recognized the expression on his friend's face—haunted, guilty, desolate. He saw it when he looked in the mirror. He'd seen it on the faces of his buddies in wartime and always there was death involved.

"What happened?"

"I was in a bar. Drunk on my ass." There was self-incrimination in Luke's voice. And biting sarcasm. "Oh, I was twenty-one. Barely."

"Then what—"

"My brothers Bailey and Daniel were with me and they were underage. It was a dive where they didn't care all that much about checking IDs." He blew out a long breath. "Bailey was twenty, Dan was only eighteen. He had more sense than his two older brothers put together."

"What happened?" It was something really bad. Brendan had lived through bad and knew what it looked like.

"Bailey was drunk, too, but Danny hadn't been drinking. He was worried that neither of us could drive home and he was right. He called the folks, figuring his macho brothers wouldn't hand over the keys to him and would try to drive."

"Was he right?"

It didn't seem possible, but Luke's face turned even more darkly intense and bleak. "We'll never know for sure."

"Why?"

"Mom and Dad were coming to deal with us but they never made it." His eyes were unbelievably sad. "They were hit and killed by a drunk driver."

Brendan had seen more than his share of violence and thought he'd heard it all. He didn't think anything could shock him but he was wrong. "Man, I'm sorry—"

"I'm not finished." Luke held up a hand. "My family was destroyed. There were seven orphans and my maternal grandparents weren't prepared to take them on. Jamie and Bella stayed together and endured the resentment of our mother's folks. The two youngest, Dana and Liza, were adopted."

Brendan thought he'd had it bad, but this man was carrying around the baggage of loved ones lost and six young lives forever changed—seven if you counted his. He recalled the day he'd met Forrest Traub and Luke talked about the plans he had for the cabins that he'd helped his dad build. Now he knew what Fiona had meant when she'd said things didn't go as planned.

"The Rust Creek Falls community looks like it comes together during hard times." He said that because he didn't know what else to say.

"They do," Luke answered. "But I left town."

"What?"

"Dan, Bailey and me. We moved out and took off. We blamed ourselves and it seemed like the best thing for the younger ones. We started out working ranches together, then split up." He looked away for a moment as painful memories seemed to scroll through his mind. "It's just in the last year or so we've reunited. We found out we owned Sunshine Farm. I was lucky to find Eva and she loved me back. On top of that she was one hundred percent on board with our vision to make this ranch mean something."

"And you're changing lives for the better, Luke."

"We're trying. So far we have a pretty good track record. Getting a reputation for bringing lonely hearts together." He smiled for the first time since walking through the door.

But Brendan wasn't smiling. He wasn't looking to be part of someone's vision. Not even for Luke's redemption. "I'm not sure why you told me all that, but—"

"Here's my point. I ran away from Rust Creek Falls. I thought I could leave it all behind me, but I was wrong. For twelve years I wrestled with the past and my guilt pinned me to the mat."

"That's not the man I see," Brendan said.

"Oh, that guy's there. And he'll always be there, carrying responsibility for what happened. I'm learning to deal. But it didn't start until I came back here and faced what I did."

Brendan dragged his fingers through his hair. "I'm sorry you went through that, but I'm still not sure why you told me. What does that have to do with me?"

"Everything. Takes one to know one. I ran away and you're running, too."

"You're wrong. This isn't where I grew up."

"No. But your run started when you joined the Marines. Now you're reenlisting. It's not hard to connect the dots." Luke's look challenged him.

"I have no idea what you're talking about." That was Bravo Sierra and Brendan knew it. Luke hit a nerve and the pain was radiating through him.

He remembered why he'd enlisted in the first place.

He couldn't wait to get away from Prosperity, Texas, and what had felt like the stigma of being different, being raised by a single dad who repaired junk for a living. He hadn't seen a lot of options and his mother had said he needed to live up to the meaning of his name. Be a warrior. So enlisting had been a way to get out from under. He'd run away.

Luke met his gaze. "I'm talking about the fact that joining the Marines was the first time you ran and going back is following the same pattern. Break it, Brendan. Stay in Rust Creek Falls. You have friends here, people who care about you. And Fiona."

He looked at the frying pan in pieces on the workbench. "I have a better chance of putting this mess back together than I do of fixing things with her."

"You don't know unless you try." Luke put a hand on his shoulder, a brotherly gesture. "There's a place for you here. We need all the help we can get with our plans for Sunshine Farm. Maybe you can do more good as a civilian and find yourself in the process."

Telling that story couldn't have been easy, Brendan thought. "I appreciate what you just did, Luke. What you told me. Thank you."

"Maybe it will help. Don't sell Fiona short. Give it a try with her. What have you got to lose?"

Everything, Brendan thought.

He watched the other man walk out the door and his mind was racing. Just a little while ago he'd been looking for the loose connection and now he knew it was him. He also knew how to fix it. He just hoped that it wasn't beyond repair.

Fiona finished hand-stitching little ears to Jared's pig costume for tonight's Halloween party at Sunshine Farm.

Her sister Fallon had called in reinforcements because caring for the triplets barely left her enough time to go to the bathroom, let alone sew costumes. Their sister Brenna came, too, and the three of them were at Short Hills Ranch.

"I can't believe the kids are still napping." Brenna raised her arms in the air, stretching after sitting hunched over to sew. "They aren't sick, are they?"

"No. Jamie helped me wear them out this morning. They were running around getting all that energy out. Then they ate lunch and crashed just before you guys got here."

"Miracles do happen." *Although not in my world*, Fiona thought. She finished sewing and held up the little piggy suit. "What do you think?"

"Absolutely adorable," Fallon said. "Mine's done, too."

"So is mine." Brenna followed their lead and put her needle and thread back in the sewing box sitting on the coffee table. "It's a good thing you were able to finish the body suits. The snout and ears were time-consuming."

Fallon gave them a grateful look. "I couldn't have done it without my sisters."

"Do you remember when Dad used to call us his three redheaded piggies?" Brenna's blue eyes sparkled.

"We were little then," Fallon reminded her.

"He wouldn't dare say that to us now," Fiona told them. Especially to her, with those extra few pounds on her hips.

She used to take exception to the family resemblance. It was impossible not to know they were sisters and inevitably people compared them. But they grew up and traveled their own paths to independent womanhood. Brenna loved being a hairdresser and making her clients look and feel pretty. She fell in love with Travis Dalton and married him.

Fallon worked at Country Kids Daycare because she'd always adored children. When Jamie was a single dad raising infant triplets, she was one of the volunteers who helped out so he could work his ranch. Romance happened and she married the rancher, became the kids' mom for real.

Fiona was the single sister and that wasn't likely to change. She hated the word *spinster*, but that's what she was. Because the man she loved was leaving town and taking her heart with him.

"What's wrong, Fee?" Fallon was sitting on the sofa beside her and looked concerned.

"Nothing."

"You just got awfully quiet." From the chair on the other side of the coffee table, Brenna looked concerned now, too.

"Just remembering the ghosts of Halloween past."

"Cute." Brenna wrinkled her adorable little nose. She put the costume she'd finished on top of the other two on the table. "Not bad if I do say so myself."

"They look great," Fallon gushed. "The Three Little Pigs. Jared, Henry and Kate are going to look so awesome in these."

"They better wake up pretty soon," Fiona said. "I want to see them dressed up and get some pictures of those rascals."

"I plan to let them sleep. They get cranky if they don't wake up on their own."

"Then I'll just stick around until they do. I'll help you get them ready," Fiona offered.

"Don't you have to get yourself into costume for the party?" Brenna scooted forward to the edge of her chair.

"Yeah," Fallon agreed. "You can see the triplets then

and get pictures. If we can keep them still long enough to take some."

"What are you dressing up as?" Brenna asked. "Do you need me to do your hair?"

Well, darn it. She'd hoped to avoid telling them face-to-face that she was skipping the party. Maybe she could just say it and her sisters wouldn't quiz her about the decision. *Right*, she thought. *When pigs could fly*.

"The thing is—" She looked at Fallon beside her, then Brenna in the chair. "I'm not going to the party."

"Why not?" her sisters said together.

She couldn't tell them the truth without crying and she really didn't want to cry. "I'm not feeling great and—"

"That's a big fat lie." Brenna pointed an accusing finger at her.

"I don't want to go," she said stubbornly.

"According to Jamie," Fallon said, "you assured Luke that you would handle the fund-raising part of the party. I've never known you to break a promise."

Darn promises anyway, she thought. She and Brendan had talked a lot about that. She knew what a broken promise felt like and that would be easier to handle than the fact that he didn't love her enough to stay. That hurt so much more.

"All the fund-raising stuff was about publicity ahead of time. I got the word out," she defended herself. "No one will miss me."

"What are we? Chopped liver?" Brenna looked at Fallon and shrugged.

Then they both stared daggers at her. The two of them reminded her of their mother, when she knew something was up and was determined to get the truth. "What?"

"This has something to do with Brendan Tanner." Fallon wasn't asking.

"Why would you think that? We're just friends." At least, he thought so. She was way beyond the friend zone.

"That's not what the Rust Creek Falls rumor mill says." Brenna sounded confident about her information. "And don't try to blow me off. I do hair. Customers talk. I hear things and gossip is almost never wrong. You've been seeing a lot of that ex-military cowboy."

"Pretty soon he won't be an ex," she said sadly. "He's reenlisting."

"No." Fallon looked shocked.

"Yes," she confirmed.

"I'm going to hurt him." Brenna's redheaded temper was showing. "Travis will help me."

"So will Jamie," Fallon vowed. "I'll make sure the triplets don't see their father defending their aunt's honor."

"You guys are sweet but Ronan already offered."

"He already knows? Before us?" Her two sisters looked stricken.

"He noticed I was upset and said he would rather have a fat lip than watch me cry."

"What do you know." Brenna sighed. "That brings a little tear to my eye. Who would have guessed our big brother is so sensitive?"

"Focus, ladies." Fallon was used to keeping the triplets in line and fell into the role of maintaining the track of this conversation. "What does his going back into the Marines have to do with you skipping out on the party?"

"That should be obvious. I don't want to see him. Especially in such a public setting. Practically everyone from Rust Creek Falls will be there."

"And you don't want to be humiliated again. Who could blame you? Well, I plan to tell Brendan that he's a weasel jerk and you're too good for him." Brenna nodded emphatically.

"That's just it. He's not a jerk. He's a really good man. This would be so much easier if he wasn't."

Fallon tapped her lip. "So, let me get this straight. Has he already put something in writing about going back in the military?"

"Not that I know of. I assume he'll do that when he's back in shape."

"You know, Josselyn Weaver was at Sunshine Farm when Brendan arrived. She saw him work out every morning and told me that man's muscles have muscles." Brenna saw the way they were looking at her. "What? I cut her hair. If she's right, he's already fit, so what's he waiting for? Why isn't he already back in uniform?"

"Fiona," her sisters prodded when she didn't answer.

"You'd have to ask him that question." Fiona shrugged. "He told me he's absolutely going back into the Marine Corps."

"And you didn't try to change his mind?"

"It was already made up," she told Fallon. "What could I say?"

"Let me think. Oh, I know. How about 'Don't go.' Or, 'I care about you.' Or, 'You'll be sorry if you let me get away.'" Fallon met her gaze. "I can think of more."

"I wouldn't stand in the way of something he really wants to do."

"Oh, please. You rolled over. That's practically show-ing him the door and shoving him out." Brenna made an exasperated sound.

"How do you know?" she protested. "You weren't there."

"I know you. Ever since that jackass toad did you wrong you give up without a fight. Wave the white flag before a shot is fired. It's as if you're expecting to get hurt so you just turn the other cheek and take it."

"Brenna's right." Fallon moved close, put an arm

around her. "If you keep pushing men away, that bastard who hurt you continues to win."

Fiona knew her sisters were right and loathed the idea of that jerk continuing to take from her. "I don't know what to do."

"Fight for him," her sisters said.

"With what?" Brendan was the warrior, not her. "I don't know how. I'm not pretty like you, Fallon, or sassy like you, Brenna."

"You're uniquely you," Fallon said gently. "And you're beautiful. One of the most lovely things about you is that you're completely unaware of how pretty and sexy you really are."

"I'd give a whole lot to have curves like you," Brenna chimed in. "Believe me, when you walk down the street, men get whiplash turning to look."

"You're my sisters. You have to say that," she objected.

"Because we're your sisters, we really don't," Brenna told her. "And maybe he's afraid."

"Oh, please," Fiona scoffed. "He's a marine."

"And he can handle himself in a military situation," Fallon agreed. "What Brenna means is that he might have personal issues that are holding him back."

"Right. We just called you on your crap," Brenna said. "Running from commitment. Could be he's doing the same thing. If one of you doesn't bend—" She sighed. "It would just be sad to waste a good thing."

"You don't have to fight. Start with the truth," Fallon suggested. "Tell him you love him. At least you'll have tried."

"I agree," Brenna said. "Explain how you feel. It will either work out or it won't. At least then you won't have regrets." She rested her elbows on her knees. "And we know how much you love Halloween. Don't let him spoil it for you."

Fiona's eyes filled with tears but this time they weren't about Brendan. "Have I ever told you guys how much I love you?"

"Sister hug." Brenna stood and walked around the table, pulling the other two into her arms.

Fiona soaked up the sibling support and decided her sisters were right. If she said nothing she was going to hurt. If she told him how she felt and he thanked her politely, then walked away, she was still going to hurt. But she wouldn't have to wonder what might have been.

Chapter Fifteen

The hardest part of putting together his Lone Ranger costume—because he was a cowboy, too—was the black mask. After talking to Luke, Brendan felt as if the mask he'd put on for so many years had been stripped away. But for the party he managed to find a black handkerchief and cut eye holes. Now he tied it and put on his Stetson, then buckled the toy gun belt he'd been lucky enough to find at Everything Old. It hadn't taken long to modify it to fit him. Tinkering was what he did, who he was, and he knew that now. If only his father was alive to see him embracing all the things he'd learned from his old man.

At the designated time, he made his way to the area in front of the big yellow barn. Earlier he'd helped Luke string white lights, put up spiderwebs and pile pumpkins. They'd also set up chairs and tables, several of which were filled with food and baked goods donated for the fund-raiser. Outdoor heaters were strategically arranged and an open area set aside for dancing later.

Already a big crowd was there and he did surveillance, looking for Fiona's bright red hair. He didn't see her and frustration knotted inside him. It was possible he'd lost the best thing that ever happened to him and had no one but himself to blame.

"Hey, Brendan."

He turned toward the male voice and smiled when he immediately recognized the man limping toward him. "It's good to see you, Forrest."

"I'm surprised you knew who I was, what with the eye patch." He was dressed up as a pirate. "What gave me away? The limp?"

Brendan laughed at the former soldier's self-deprecating humor. There wasn't a trace of bitterness in his tone or expression and he knew there had been once.

"I hate to be the one to tell you this, but the eye patch doesn't hide all that much of your face."

"Back at you, buddy. When you ride off into the sunset, no one will be asking 'Who was that masked man?'"

"Oh, please, Forrest, everyone knows the Lone Ranger." The woman with him, dressed as Princess Leia, looked up teasingly.

Forrest smiled at the pretty, brown-eyed brunette. "Brendan Tanner, I'd like you to meet my beautiful wife, Angie."

She held out her hand. "It's really nice to meet you."

"Same here."

They chatted about the fund-raiser, this community's generosity and Thunder Canyon, where the couple was from. Brendan thought about all the people he'd met since arriving here. Every one of them had acted as if they'd known him forever. Treated him like one of their own. It reminded him of the Marine Corps without the deployments. And he'd decided to walk away. Someone should stamp Idiot on his forehead. And damn, he still didn't see Fiona.

With an effort Brendan pulled his thoughts back to

what Angie Traub had said. "It's really a good thing that Luke is doing here. For people in general, but veterans, too."

"Returning service members have a lot of needs." Forrest was serious now. "And not just those recovering from wounds or PTSD. Integrating into civilian life has its own challenges. Navigating government benefits programs can be confusing. We need support groups and volunteers to run interference for them."

Brendan remembered what Luke had said about him being able to do more good in civilian life. Maybe he was right.

Speaking of Luke, he walked over to them and gave Angie a kiss on the cheek then shook hands with Forrest. "Thanks for coming."

"We wouldn't miss this," the other man said.

Luke nodded with satisfaction as he stood in front of the wide-open yellow barn doors and gazed at all the people gathered in front of them. Most in costume. Some not. "There are more folks here than I'd even hoped."

"Obviously Fiona did a great job of getting the word out," Forrest observed. "I haven't seen her yet. Have you?"

"No." Brendan had been constantly scouting the crowd. "Maybe she couldn't make it."

"I don't think so." Luke shook his head. "You can count on Fiona."

Even if some jerk broke her heart, Brendan thought. "So you're sure she'll be here?"

"Yes." Not a shred of doubt in Luke's voice. "But it's time for me to make some welcoming remarks to everyone."

He tried to get the crowd's attention without success. When the talking didn't stop, he let loose with a shrill whistle that could probably be heard all the way to Prosperity, Texas.

When there was quiet Luke said, "My wife and I would like to thank you all for coming tonight. Where are you, Eva?"

"Over here," she called. Everyone looked at Raggedy Ann behind the dessert table, collecting money for the donated baked goods.

"I won't bore you for long, but I want to say just a few words." After applause, whistles and catcalls receded, Luke continued, "When we discovered that we owned this place it felt like a fresh start for me and my family.

"Right now there are seven cabins. The idea is to give people who are looking for something, a different perspective on their life, a fresh start or whatever… This is a place to figure things out."

Brendan was watching the people listening attentively to every word. They were nodding enthusiastically and flashing thumbs-up.

"It's working out so well, I want to take things to the next level. Expand. That takes money, so tonight I'm announcing that this is the first annual fund-raiser for the Lauren and Rob Stockton Memorial Foundation—"

Applause interrupted him but emotion had already stopped his speech. Brendan could see Luke fighting for control. A brother had a brother's back. Brendan wasn't a talker, but he jumped in now. Because a friend needed backup.

"I reached out to Luke during a rough time in my life. I left a career in the Marine Corps that I loved because my father was diagnosed with cancer and I wanted to help him fight it. We lost that battle and another one started for me. I had to figure out what I wanted to do with my life, figure out where I fit. Without hesitation, Luke offered me one of the cabins. He became more than a friend and Rust Creek Falls turned out to be so much more than somewhere to stay for a while—"

Just then the crowd shifted a little and he saw Fiona. The Three Little Pigs surrounded her and he knew they had to be the triplets. They were cute, but he only had eyes for her. She was wearing black and had on a pointy witch hat. Her face was painted green and he wasn't even sure how he knew it was her. But he did.

His heart started hammering as fear and hope twisted together inside him. First he had to get through his talk. "Now Luke wants to build more cabins, help more people and set aside a couple specifically for veterans. I think some of them can lend a hand to the project while they're here dealing with their personal challenges. Honest labor for a good cause could make them feel useful, a part of something." Brendan knew that firsthand and looked at Luke, who nodded his approval. He could take over now. "So it's time for him to twist your arm for money."

Luke laughed and put a hand on his shoulder. "Thanks, Brendan. And you're right. This is the part where I ask for money. There's a bake sale going on and a donation jar." He shaded his eyes from the lights hitting him and scanned the crowd. "I see some of the Jones family out there. Just so we're clear, I expect you billionaire boys to dig deep."

Brendan heard a bit of good-natured grumbling from somewhere at the back of the crowd but all he could think about was Fiona. He needed to get to her. But when people moved back and forth again, she'd disappeared. Damn it.

"With your help, we can make this project a reality," Luke said. "Now, Eva and I want everyone to have fun."

Brendan started to walk away but Luke put a hand on

his arm. "Hey, thanks for stepping in. I didn't expect to choke up like that."

"I owe you more than I can ever repay. It was the least I could do."

"So, can I read into what you said? Are you planning to stick around Rust Creek Falls, after all?"

"That's what I'd like to know." The female voice came from behind him.

Brendan would recognize it anywhere—soft and sexy and full of sass. He turned and stared at her green face. "Fiona."

"Hey, Fee," Luke said. "I'd give you a hug but I don't want any of that green stuff on me. Good job with the publicity."

"Happy to do it." She let out a long breath, then squared her shoulders. "I need to talk to Brendan. Would you mind terribly giving us some—"

"Space?" Luke filled in as he turned to walk away. "There's nothing else I would rather do."

Fiona could hardly breathe. So, this was happening. She looked at Brendan, trying to read the expression on his face. It wasn't like the mask over his eyes actually hid anything but she had no idea what he was thinking.

"Fiona, I—"

Someone bumped into her, propelling her against him. Brendan's arms came around her and felt more wonderful than she remembered. She wanted to stay there forever but that wasn't what he wanted. So, this time when she was left behind, she was determined to have no regrets about getting stuff off her chest.

"Follow me," she said, stepping away from him. "We have to talk."

She'd been publicly humiliated once; it wouldn't happen again. She wanted privacy for what she had to say. That way when she broke down, no one else had to know.

Except suddenly her family was there—Ronan and Keegan, her parents. Fallon and Jamie. Brenna and Travis. The adults were kind of looking fiercely at him. But he ignored that and hunkered down, focusing on the triplets.

"You guys look awesome."

Jared pointed to himself. "Me piggy."

"I can see that." Brendan playfully grabbed the boy up into his arms and Jared squealed with delight. "Watch out for the big bad wolf. He'll huff and puff and—"

"Blow your house down," little Kate finished. She threw her arms around his jeans-clad leg.

"Me, too. Want up." Henry held out his arms to get in on the action.

Fiona wasn't quite sure how, but he had all three toddlers in his arms. He was growling playfully while the kids giggled and shrieked.

Finally Jared had enough. "I hungry. Want a cupcake, Mommy."

"Let's get some real food first," Fallon said. When the kids were grounded again she took two little hands in hers and let her husband get Jared. Then she gave Brendan a hard stare. "You're a complete moron."

"No name-calling, sweetheart," her mother said. "Use positive words in front of the children. Let's go find the food."

"I can't think of one that is more perfect than—" Fallon glanced at her kids, then spelled, *"M-o-r-o-n."*

"And you're not wrong," Paddy agreed. The look he gave Brendan could scorch paint and it seemed as if there would be more to say, but he followed after his wife and daughter.

Brenna gave him a long, hostile stare. "If you know what's good for you—"

"I think he gets the message, honey." Travis put his hand to her back and urged her forward. He shook his head and said, "Poor bastard."

Ronan and Keegan stood side by side, looking like twin bodyguards. Fiona loved them for it but this was her deal. "I want to talk to him. I've got this, guys."

"You sure?" Ronan looked skeptical.

"We don't mind sticking around," Keegan added.

In spite of the nerves quivering inside her and the sadness pushing them out of the way, Fiona smiled at her two brothers. For a split second, love for these big lugs squeezed out everything messy and complicated. "Thanks. But I really do have this."

With a last warning look, the two men waded through the crowd and headed toward the tables where food and drink were set up.

"Okay, then." She looked up at Brendan and said again, "Follow me."

"Are you sure that's all of them?" he asked warily.

"Yes. At least the ones I'm related to," she answered. "But I can't guarantee my town family won't have something to say to you."

"I'm not sure whether to be happy about that for your sake or very afraid." He grabbed her hand and led the way through the partygoers gathered outside and past the perimeter of light.

Fiona didn't care where he took her because his big, warm hand felt so good wrapped around hers. But she pushed the thought away. This was no time to go soft. There were things she needed to tell him and hardened herself for the conversation.

It didn't take long to see that they were heading for his

cabin. About that hardening her heart thing? No way she would end up in his bed. Not again.

He stepped onto the porch of his place and released her hand. "We can talk in here."

As long as they just talked. This would very probably be the last time she was with him and it would be so easy to let herself forget that she wasn't enough to make him stay.

"Okay." She walked through the door he opened and flipped on the light switch just inside.

As the room lit up, memories flooded her. The best times of her life had happened here. She hoped that eventually thoughts of being with him would be warm, bright and comforting. Right now it just hurt all the way to her soul. When the door closed, she blinked away tears and turned to face him.

He stared at her for a moment. "So…the green face is really something."

She touched her cheek, a little sticky from the face paint she'd used. "Yeah. I didn't want to be any old generic witch."

"So, which witch are you?"

"Elphaba." His look was blank. "From the Broadway play *Wicked*."

He shrugged. "Still nothing."

"I'm sure you can find something about it on YouTube."

"I'll check it out."

"'Defying Gravity' is my favorite song from the play. But my second fave is 'For Good'—"

As soon as the words came out of her mouth, the meaning sliced through her painfully. Because she'd known him she'd been changed for good. Fiona was aware of how awesome it was to be in love. Also because she'd known him it felt as if her heart was being ripped out. At least this time she would get closure.

"You didn't really want to talk to me about a play, did you?" His voice was so gentle she could hardly stand it.

"No." She caught the corner of her bottom lip between her teeth for a moment. "I just thought we should talk about what you told me."

"Yeah." He moved a step closer until his body nearly touched hers. "I didn't like the way we left things, either. And that's my fault. You mentioned your family and—"

"I know. They can be a lot."

"It's not that. They're great. Especially the way they support you. My dad was all the family I had. And you have so many of them."

"You're trying to say that I take them for granted," she said.

"Not exactly. I'm saying that I envy you. I didn't have any siblings. My mom wasn't around for putting together a costume or going trick-or-treating."

"Brendan—" She sighed. "I'm so sorry you had to go through that."

"Me, too. But I'm really not feeling sorry for myself. I just need you to understand why the Marine Corps is so important to me. They were the brothers I never had. The family I never had. I knew I could count on them."

"You can count on me."

He looked away. "I know—"

"It's not just lip service, Brendan. I have your back always." It was now or never. "I'm in love with you."

His eyes met hers and he blinked at her. "Fiona—"

She held up a hand to stop his words. "Let me get this out before I lose my nerve. I fell in love with you. Couldn't help it. I love you for trying to keep your distance in order to protect me. It just shows what kind of man you are." She shrugged. "And it's a perfect example of why I fell hard for you."

"Listen, Fiona—"

"I'm not asking you for anything. I just wanted you to know." She took in his handsome face, including the black mask, and smiled. "I like the Lone Ranger thing you've got going on. Very heroic."

"I'm not a hero."

"You served your country, bravely and honorably. You're everyone's hero."

"I don't care about everyone. I only want to be your hero." He shook his head. "I was afraid you weren't coming tonight."

"I almost didn't," she admitted. "My sisters talked me into it. They said I should tell you how I feel."

"I'm glad you did and now it's my turn." He untied the black mask and took off his hat, then tossed both on the couch. "I've been hiding all my life. From pain and possibility. I've been running and hiding because that's where I'm comfortable. But not anymore. Not if it means losing you."

His words seeded hope that started to grow in her heart. "What are you saying?"

"I love you. I have from the very first moment I saw you. Chasing Jared into my workshop."

"You have no idea how badly I want to throw myself into your arms right now."

"What's stopping you?"

"You are." Love was all well and good, but logistics sucked. "Or I should say the fact that you're going to re-enlist."

"No. I'm not."

She shook her head. "Don't do that. Don't you dare

give up the career you love. Not for me. I won't push you into a commitment you don't want."

"I'm not doing it for you," he protested. "I'm doing it for me. There's nothing more important to me than being with you. Because I'm in love with you. And I'm not giving up anything. I've been talking to Forrest Traub, and there are other ways for me to serve. I can do a lot. It just won't be on the front lines anymore."

"You're sure? I don't want you to resent me." Fiona searched his face, looking for any sign of doubt. She saw nothing but love in his eyes. And this was the man who never broke a promise and always told the truth.

"I want to be with *you*. I want to walk in the snow for the first time with you. Thanksgiving and Christmas were always another holiday to have hard feelings about. Now I can't wait to spend them with you." He reached for her.

Fiona took a half step back. "What about my family? You saw how they are. They're going to be around."

He laughed and the humor lines crinkled around his eyes. "I was completely serious when I said I envy you having a big family. I would very much like to be a part of the rowdy O'Reillys. I'd like nothing more."

"Nothing?" she asked sweetly.

"Nothing." He pulled her into his arms then. "Except maybe to start a family of my own. With you. If you'll have me."

She cupped his lean cheek in her hand. "You are everything I have ever wanted, Brendan Tanner."

He kissed her then, and she slid her arms around his neck. When they came up for air, she said, "You've got green face paint all over you."

There was a wicked gleam in his eyes when he glanced

in the direction of the bedroom, then back at her. "I propose we make it count, then."

"I'm in." She stood on tiptoe and kissed him softly. "Always."

Epilogue

"There should be a medal I can pin on you for meritorious service." Fiona pulled the tablecloth off the dining room table. After a holiday dinner the thing looked like it had been through a battle. She smiled at Brendan. "You just survived your first O'Reilly family Thanksgiving."

"Marine Corps boot camp came in handy. I never knew it would prepare me for taking on triplet toddlers."

"They adore you." The sight of him playing and roughhousing with the kids had tugged at her heart. Partly because what woman didn't love watching a hunky man with kids? But mostly because he'd looked so happy.

Now the two of them were clearing away Thanksgiving decorations so her mother could get out the ones for Christmas. It would be her first with Brendan. He had wandered over to the front window and was staring at something so she decided to join him.

"What are you looking at?"

"It's snowing." There was awe in his voice and something else she'd never heard before. When he looked down at her there was a gleam in his eyes, too. The excitement of seeing his first snowfall? "Will you take a walk with me?"

"Anywhere." She leaned her head against his shoulder for a moment. "Let's get our coats."

They grabbed sheepskin-lined jackets from the coat rack by the front door and tugged them on.

"Ready," she said.

"Are you sure?" There was a funny look on his face.

"Is something wrong?"

"No."

"I mean, this is your first snow and everything, but I promise I'll take care of you," she teased.

"Not a doubt in my mind that you have my six." He stuck his hand in the pocket of his jacket and seemed to relax. "I'm ready."

She grinned and opened the front door, letting in a draft of cold air. Light from the front window showed big fat, wet flakes of snow gently falling. It was slowly accumulating on the ground and turning the front yard into a white wonderland. It was magical.

"Let's go." She took his hand. "Remember it's slippery."

They walked down the steps and wandered slowly away from the house. Peace and quiet surrounded them. It felt as if they were the only two people in the world. Since Halloween her love for this man had only grown stronger, deeper. Watching him enthusiastically immerse himself in the community filled her heart with happiness until it overflowed. She couldn't imagine her life without him in it.

She tucked her left hand into the bend of his elbow and he covered it with his own, brushing his thumb over her fingers.

"Can I ask you something?" she said.

"Anything," he answered without hesitation.

"Do you regret giving up the military?"

"No." Again there was no hesitation.

"Are you sure?" she asked. "Now that you've had a few weeks to think about it. You're not sorry you didn't reenlist?"

"I haven't had time to be sorry." He looked down and there was contentment in his eyes, in his expression. "I'm partnering with Luke in the Sunshine Farm Fix-it Shop. He's taken to calling me the tractor whisperer and the backhoe badass."

"I'm not sure whether to be horrified at the nicknames or impressed that Luke is so impressed."

"I vote for impressed." Then he continued, "On top of that, I'm organizing a group of veteran volunteers with construction experience to help build cabins. And we're going to negotiate the details of renting a space at Everything Old to sell donated items I've repaired in order to raise money for Luke's foundation."

"You're going to be busy."

"That's the way I like it," he said. "And I've told you about all this. So what's wrong?"

"I just want to make sure you haven't changed your mind. About staying, I mean."

"Why in the world would I?" He stopped walking and smiled down at her. "I'm happier than I've ever been in my life. Don't look now, but we're one more positive story in the growing myth of the Lonelyhearts Ranch."

"Yeah." She grinned. "Fiona and Brendan—the legend continues."

His expression turned serious then. "You look so beautiful with snow sticking to your eyelashes and in your hair. I'm glad you're my first walk in the snow."

"I'm glad you're glad." She smiled. "There was a time when I was practically obsessed with getting married because my sisters were. I was the oldest and should have been first down the aisle."

"And now?"

"Love is the most important thing. I'm okay with being a thirty-year-old spinster. As long as I can be *your* thirty-year-old spinster."

"Don't get used to the spinster thing." Suddenly he dropped to one knee and reached a hand into his jacket pocket.

Her heart started hammering. "Brendan? What are you doing? Snow is cold, you know. And wet. You're going to get frostbite of the kneecap. This is crazy. Please stand up before you catch your death—"

"If you'll stop talking and let me get a word in, I have something to ask you."

"Okay. Stopping. Now—"

"Fiona—"

She pressed her lips together and he pulled a black velvet jeweler's box from his pocket, opened it and took out a solitaire diamond ring.

"I love you more than anything in this world and want to spend the rest of my life with you. Fiona O'Reilly—"

"Can I say yes now?"

"I haven't asked you anything yet," he said.

"So hurry up," she urged.

"Will you marry me?"

"Yes." She stuck out her left hand. "It would be my honor to marry you, Brendan Tanner."

He slipped the ring on her finger and kissed her hand. Looking up at her he said, "You're the best thing that ever happened to me."

"And you're the best thing that ever happened to me. Let's go break the news to my family."

"I think they already know." He nodded toward the house, where her parents, her siblings and their families were peeking through the window, waving and giving them thumbs-up.

She sighed. "Get used to it. For better for worse. Take me, take the O'Reillys."

"Gladly." He stood and pulled her against him.

Fiona threw her arms around his neck. Waking up that morning, she'd had no idea she would find even more to be thankful for. The list was long, but now, right at the top, was living happily-ever-after with her marine.

* * * * *

SPECIAL EXCERPT FROM

HQN™

Turn the page for a sneak peek at New York Times
*bestselling author RaeAnne Thayne's next
heartwarming Haven Point romance,*
Season of Wonder,
available October 2018 from HQN Books!

*Dani Capelli and her daughters are
facing their first Christmas in Haven Point.
But Ruben Morales—the son of Dani's new boss—is
determined to give them a season of wonder!*

CHAPTER ONE

"THIS IS TOTALLY LAME. Why do we have to stay here and wait for you? We can walk home in, like, ten minutes."

Daniela Capelli drew in a deep breath and prayed for patience, something she seemed to be doing with increasing frequency these days when it came to her thirteen-year-old daughter. "It's starting to snow and already almost dark."

Silver rolled her eyes, something *she* did with increasing frequency these days. "So what? A little snow won't kill us. I would hardly even call that snow. We had way bigger storms than this back in Boston. Remember that big blizzard a few years ago, when school was closed for, like, a week?"

"I remember," her younger daughter, Mia, said, looking up from her coloring book at Dani's desk at the Haven Point Veterinary Clinic. "I stayed home from preschool and I watched Anna and Elsa a thousand times, until you said your eardrums would explode if I played it one more time."

Dani could hear a bark from the front office that likely signaled the arrival of her next client and knew she didn't have time to stand here arguing with an obstinate teenager.

"Mia can't walk as fast as you can. You'll end up frustrated with her and you'll both be freezing before you make it home," she pointed out.

"So she can stay here and wait for you while I walk home. I just told Chelsea we could FaceTime about the new dress she bought and she can only do it for another hour before her dad comes to pick her up for his visitation."

"Why can't you FaceTime here? I only have two more patients to see. I'll be done in less than an hour, then we can all go home together. You can hang out in the waiting room with Mia, where the Wi-Fi signal is better."

Silver gave a huge put-upon sigh but picked up her backpack and stalked out of Dani's office toward the waiting room.

"Can I turn on the TV out there?" Mia asked as she gathered her papers and crayons. "I like the dog shows."

The veterinary clinic showed calming clips of animals on a big flat-screen TV set low to the ground for their clientele.

"After Silver's done with her phone call, okay?"

"She'll take *forever*," Mia predicted with a gloomy look. "She always does when she's talking to Chelsea."

Dani fought to hide a smile. "Thanks for your patience, sweetie, with her and with me. Finish your math worksheet while you're here, then when we get home, you can watch what you want."

Both the Haven Point elementary and middle schools

were within walking distance of the clinic and it had become a habit for Silver to walk to the elementary school and then walk with Mia to the clinic to spend a few hours until they could all go home together.

Of late, Silver had started to complain that she didn't want to pick her sister up at the elementary school every day, that she would rather they both just took their respective school buses home, where Silver could watch her sister without having to hang out at the boring veterinary clinic.

This working professional/single mother gig was *hard*, she thought as she ushered Mia to the waiting room. Then again, in most ways it was much easier than the veterinary student/single mother gig had been.

When they entered the comfortable waiting room— with its bright colors, pet-friendly benches and big fish tank—Mia faltered for a moment, then sidestepped behind Dani's back.

She saw instantly what had caused her daughter's nervous reaction. Funny. Dani felt the same way. She wanted to hide behind somebody, too.

The receptionist had given her the files with the dogs' names that were coming in for a checkup but hadn't mentioned their human was Ruben Morales. Her gorgeous next-door neighbor.

Dani's palms instantly itched and her stomach felt as if she'd accidentally swallowed a flock of butterflies.

"Deputy Morales," she said, then paused, hating the slightly breathless note in her voice.

What *was* it about the man that always made her so freaking nervous?

He was big, yes, at least six feet tall, with wide shoulders, tough muscles and a firm, don't-mess-with-me jawline.

It wasn't just that. Even without his uniform, the man exuded authority and power, which instantly raised her hackles and left her uneasy, something she found both frustrating and annoying about herself.

No matter how far she had come, how hard she had worked to make a life for her and her girls, she still sometimes felt like the troublesome foster kid from Queens.

She had done her best to avoid him in the months they had been in Haven Point, but that was next to impossible when they lived so close to each other—and when she was the intern in his father's veterinary practice.

"Hey, Doc," he said, flashing her an easy smile she didn't trust for a moment. It never quite reached his dark, long-lashed eyes, at least where she was concerned.

While she might be uncomfortable around Ruben Morales, his dogs were another story.

He held the leashes of both of them, a big, muscular Belgian shepherd and an incongruously paired little Chipoo, and she reached down to pet both of them. They sniffed her and wagged happily, the big dog's tail nearly knocking over his small friend.

That was the thing she loved most about dogs. They were uncomplicated and generous with their affection, for the most part. They never looked at people with that subtle hint of suspicion, as if trying to uncover all their secrets.

"I wasn't expecting you," she admitted.

"Oh? I made an appointment. The boys both need checkups. Yukon needs his regular hip and eye check and Ollie is due for his shots."

She gave the dogs one more pat before she straightened and faced him, hoping his sharp cop eyes couldn't notice evidence of her accelerated pulse.

"Your father is still here every Monday and Friday afternoons. Maybe you should reschedule with him," she suggested. It was a faint hope, but a girl had to try.

"Why would I do that?"

"Maybe because he's your father and knows your dogs?"

"Dad is an excellent veterinarian. Agreed. But he's also semiretired and wants to be fully retired this time next year. As long as you plan to stick around in Haven Point, we will have to switch vets and start seeing you eventually. I figured we might as well start now."

He was checking her out. Not *her* her, but her skills as a veterinarian.

The implication was clear. She had been here three months, and it had become obvious during that time in their few interactions that Ruben Morales was extremely protective of his family. He had been polite enough when they had met previously, but always with a certain guardedness, as if he was afraid she planned to take the good name his hardworking father had built up over the years for the Haven Point Veterinary Clinic and drag it through the sludge at the bottom of Lake Haven.

Dani pushed away her instinctive prickly defensiveness, bred out of all those years in foster care when she felt as if she had no one else to count on—compounded by the difficult years after she married Tommy and had Silver, when she *really* had no one else in her corner.

She couldn't afford to offend Ruben. She didn't need his protective wariness to turn into full-on suspicion. With a little digging, Ruben could uncover things about her and her past that would ruin everything for her and her girls here.

She forced a professional smile. "It doesn't matter. Let's go back to a room and take a look at these guys.

Girls, I'll be done shortly. Silver, keep an eye on your sister."

Her oldest nodded without looking up from her phone and with an inward sigh, Dani led the way to the largest of the exam rooms.

She stood at the door as he entered the room with the two dogs, then joined him inside and closed it behind her.

The large room seemed to shrink unnaturally and she paused inside for a moment, flustered and wishing she could escape. Dani gave herself a mental shake. She could handle being in the same room with the one man in Haven Point who left her breathless and unsteady.

All she had to do was focus on the reason he was here in the first place. His dogs.

She knelt to their level. "Hey there, guys. Who wants to go first?"

The Malinois wagged his tail again while his smaller counterpoint sniffed around her shoes, probably picking up the scents of all the other dogs she had seen that day.

"Ollie, I guess you're the winner today."

He yipped, his big ears that stuck straight out from his face quivering with excitement.

He was the funniest-looking dog, quirky and unique, with wisps of fur in odd places, spindly legs and a narrow Chihuahua face. She found him unbearably cute. With that face, she wouldn't ever be able to say no to him if he were hers.

"Can I give him a treat?" She always tried to ask permission first from her clients' humans.

"Only if you want him to be your best friend for life," Ruben said.

Despite her nerves, his deadpan voice sparked a smile, which widened when she gave the little dog one of the treats she always carried in the pocket of her lab coat. He slurped it up in one bite, then sat with a resigned sort of patience during the examination.

She was aware of Ruben watching her as she carefully examined the dog, but Dani did her best not to let his scrutiny fluster her.

She knew what she was doing, she reminded herself. She had worked so hard to be here, sacrificing all her time, energy and resources of the last decade to nothing else but her girls and her studies.

"Everything looks good," she said after checking out the dog and finding nothing unusual. "He seems like a healthy little guy. It says here he's about six or seven. So you haven't had him from birth?"

"No. Only about two years. He was a stray I picked up off the side of the road between here and Shelter Springs when I was on patrol one day. He was in a bad way, half-starved, fur matted. As small as he is, it's a wonder he wasn't picked off by a coyote or even one of the bigger hawks. He just needed a little TLC."

"You couldn't find his owner?"

"We ran ads and Dad checked with all his contacts at shelters and veterinary clinics from here to Boise with no luck. I had been fostering him while we looked, and to be honest, I kind of lost my heart to the little guy, and by then Yukon adored him so we decided to keep him."

She was such a sucker for animal lovers, especially those who rescued the vulnerable and lost ones.

And, no, she didn't need counseling to point out the parallels to her own life.

Regardless, she couldn't let herself be drawn to Ruben and risk doing something foolish. She had too much to lose here in Haven Point.

"What about Yukon here?" She knelt down to examine the bigger dog. In her experience, sometimes bigger dogs didn't like to be lifted and she wasn't sure if the beautiful Malinois fell into that category.

Ruben shrugged as he scooped Ollie onto his lap to keep the little Chi-poo from swooping in and stealing the treat she held out for the bigger dog. "You could say he was a rescue, too."

"Oh?"

"He was a K-9 officer down in Mountain Home. After his handler was killed in the line of duty, I guess he kind of went into a canine version of depression and wouldn't work with anyone else. I know that probably sounds crazy."

She scratched the dog's ears, touched by the bond that could build between handler and dog. "Not at all," she said briskly. "I've seen many dogs go into decline when their owners die. It's not uncommon."

"For a year or so, they tried to match him up with other officers, but things never quite gelled, for one reason or another, then his eyes started going. His previous handler who died was a good buddy of mine from the academy, and I couldn't let him go just anywhere."

"Retired police dogs don't always do well in civilian life. They can be aggressive with other dogs and some-times people. Have you had any problems with that?"

"Not with Yukon. He's friendly. Aren't you, buddy? You're a good boy."

Dani could swear the dog grinned at his owner, his tongue lolling out.

Yukon was patient while she looked him over, espe-cially as she maintained a steady supply of treats.

When she finished, she gave the dog a pat and stood. "Can I take a look at Ollie's ears one more time?"

"Sure. Help yourself."

He held the dog out and she reached for Ollie. As she

did, the dog wriggled a little, and Dani's hands ended up brushing Ruben's chest. She froze at the accidental contact, a shiver rippling down her spine. She pinned her reaction on the undeniable fact that it had been entirely too long since she had touched a man, even accidentally.

She had to cut out this *fascination* or whatever it was immediately. Clean-cut, muscular cops were *not* her type, and the sooner she remembered that the better.

She focused on checking the ears of the little dog, gave him one more scratch and handed him back to Ruben. "That should do it. A clean bill of health. You obviously take good care of them."

He patted both dogs with an affectionate smile that did nothing to ease her nerves.

"My dad taught me well. I spent most of my youth helping out here at the clinic—cleaning cages, brushing coats, walking the occasional overnight boarder. Whatever grunt work he needed. He made all of us help."

"I can think of worse ways to earn a dime," she said.

The chance to work with animals would have been a dream opportunity for her, back when she had few bright spots in her world.

"So can I. I always loved animals."

She had to wonder why he didn't follow in his father's footsteps and become a vet. If he had, she probably wouldn't be here right now, as Frank Morales probably would have handed down his thriving practice to his own progeny.

Not that it was any of her business. Ruben certainly could follow any career path he wanted—as long as that path took him far away from her.

"Give me a moment to grab those medications and I'll be right back."

"No rush."

Out in the hall, she closed the door behind her and drew in a deep breath.

Get a grip, she chided herself. *He's just a hot-looking dude. Heaven knows you've had more than enough experience with those to last a lifetime.*

She went to the well-stocked medication dispensary, found what she needed and returned to the exam room.

Outside the door, she paused for only a moment to gather her composure before pushing it open. "Here are the pills for Ollie's nerves and a refill for Yukon's eyedrops," she said briskly. "Let me know if you have any questions—though if you do, you can certainly ask your father."

"Thanks." As he took them from her, his hands brushed hers again and sent a little spark of awareness shivering through her.

She was probably imagining the way his gaze sharpened, as if he had felt something odd, too.

"I can show you out. We're shorthanded today since the veterinary tech and the receptionist both needed to leave early."

"No problem. That's what I get for scheduling the last appointment of the day—though, again, I spent most of my youth here. I think we can find our way."

"It's fine. I'll show you out." She stood outside the door while he gathered the dogs' leashes, then led the way toward the front office.

After three months, Ruben still couldn't get a bead on Dr. Daniela Capelli.

His next-door neighbor still seemed a complete enigma to him. By all reports from his father, she was a dedicated, earnest new veterinarian with a knack for solving difficult medical mysteries and a willingness to work hard. She seemed like a warm and loving mother, at least from the few times he had seen her interactions with her two girls, the uniquely named teenager Silver—who had, paradoxically, purple hair—and the sweet-as-Christmas-toffee Mia, who was probably about six.

He also couldn't deny she was beautiful, with slender features, striking green eyes, dark, glossy hair and a dusky skin tone that proclaimed her Italian heritage—as if her name didn't do the trick first.

He actually liked the trace of New York accent that slipped into her speech at times. It fitted her somehow, in a way he couldn't explain. Despite that, he couldn't deny that the few times he had interacted with more than a wave in passing, she was brusque, prickly and sometimes downright distant.

His father adored her and wouldn't listen to a negative thing about her.

You just have to get to know her, Frank had said the other night. He apparently didn't see how diligently Dani Capelli worked to keep anyone else from doing just that.

She wasn't unfriendly, only distant. She kept herself to herself. Did Dani have any idea how fascinated the people of Haven Point were with these new arrivals in their midst?

Or maybe that was just him.

As he followed her down the hall in her white lab coat, his dogs behaving themselves for once, Ruben told himself to forget about his stupid attraction to her.

When they walked into the clinic waiting room, they found her two girls there. The older one was texting on her phone while her sister did somersaults around the room.

Dani stopped in the doorway and seemed to swallow an exasperated sound. "Mia, honey, you're going to have dog hair all over you."

"I'm a snowball rolling down the hill," the girl said. "Can't you see me getting bigger and bigger and bigger?"

He could tell the moment the little girl spotted him and his dogs coming into the area behind her mother. She went still and then slowly rose to her feet, features shifting from gleeful to nervous.

Why was she so afraid of him?

"You make a very good snowball," he said, pitching his voice low and calm as his father had taught him to do with all skittish creatures. "I haven't seen anybody somersault that well in a long time."

She moved to her mother's side and buried her face in Dani's white coat—though he didn't miss the way she reached down to pet Ollie on her way.

"Hey again, Silver."

He knew the older girl from the middle school, where he served as the resource officer a few hours a week. He made it a point to learn all the students' names and tried to talk to them individually when he had the chance, in hopes that if they had a problem they would feel comfortable coming to him.

He had the impression that Silver was like her mother in many ways. Reserved, wary, slow to trust. It made him wonder just who had hurt them.

Don't miss Season of Wonder
by RaeAnne Thayne,
available October 2018
wherever HQN books and ebooks are sold!

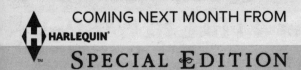

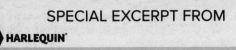
How hadn't he heard her first knock?

And then she saw the carrier on the chair next to him. He'd been rocking it.

"What on earth are you doing to that baby?" she exclaimed, nothing in mind but to rescue the child in obvious distress.

"Damned if I know," he said loudly enough to be heard over the noise. "I fed her, burped her, changed her. I've done everything they said to do, but she won't stop crying."

Tamara was already unbuckling the strap that held the crying infant in her seat. She was so tiny! Couldn't have been more than a few days old. There were no tears on her cheeks.

"There's nothing poking her. I checked," Collins said, not interfering as she lifted the baby from the seat, careful to support the little head.

It wasn't until that warm weight settled against her that Tamara realized what she'd done. She was holding a baby. Something she couldn't do.

She was going to pay. With a hellacious nightmare at the very least.

The baby's cries had stopped as soon as Tamara picked her up.

"What did you do?" Collins was there, practically touching her, he was standing so close.

"Nothing. I picked her up."

"There must've been some problem with the seat, after all…" He'd tossed the infant head support on the desk and was removing the washable cover.

"I'm guessing she just wanted to be held," Tamara said. What the hell was she doing?

Tearless crying generally meant anger, not physical distress. And why did Flint Collins have a baby in his office?

She had to put the child down. But couldn't until he put the seat back together. The newborn's eyes were closed and she hiccuped and then sighed.

Clenching her lips for a second, Tamara looked away. "Babies need to be held almost as much as they need to be fed," she told him while she tried to understand what was going on.

He was checking the foam beneath the seat cover and the straps, too. He was fairly distraught himself.

Not what she would've predicted from a hard-core businessman possibly stealing from her father.

"Who is she?" she asked, figuring it was best to start at the bottom and work her way up to exposing him for the thief he probably was.

He straightened. Stared at the baby in her arms, his brown eyes softening and yet giving away a hint of what looked like fear at the same time. In that second she wished like hell that her father was wrong and Collins wouldn't turn out to be the one who was stealing from Owens Investments.

Don't miss
An Unexpected Christmas Baby *by Tara Taylor Quinn,*
available November 2018 wherever
Harlequin® Special Edition books and ebooks are sold.

www.Harlequin.com